THE LURKING GUN

For days the two riders had been on Jim Gary's trail. With his wound not yet healed and the fever still on him, Jim couldn't keep away from them much longer. And then he sighted the town of Antler just when it looked impossible to continue.

Maybe it meant his luck was changing. Maybe he could put the gun-packing duo off his trail, get some rest, and then break away in a different direction . . .

But fate had played a grim joke. He could forget the men on his trail all right, because Antler, Nevada, was all primed to become Jim Gary's Boot Hill.

THE LURKING GUN

Clement Hardin

GUNSMOKE

This hardback edition 2008
by BBC Audiobooks Ltd
by arrangement with
Golden West Literary Agency

ISBN 978 1 405 68251 0

Printed and bound in Great Britain by
CPI Antony Rowe, Chippenham, Wiltshire

I

IT WAS the storm that finally stopped Jim Gary. It came blowing in after him, as the long trail brought him into this nameless Nevada town at an hour past midnight. Lightning flickered with an eye-punishing steadiness. When his tired Swallowfork buckskin carried him across the bridge at the north end of the settlement, its hoofs thudding hollowly on the plankings, the wind swelled suddenly to pummel the trees that lined the shallow wash below. Gary stopped in the middle of the bridge, and turned in his saddle for a long look into the uneasy darkness at his back.

No rain, yet, but it was bound to let go in a matter of minutes. The town had battened down against the coming weather; its doors and windows were shut and showed few lights. He had a feeling of being the only living thing abroad in this night of sound and wind fury, and the thought filled him with a great weariness. Yet, as he stared with burning eyes back along the trail, he knew well enough that the Planks were only hours behind him.

That day a high shoulder had given him a long rearward view and showed the pair of them, black dots moving against the tawny sweep of trail. Jim Gary knew they'd seen him too, of course. After a week of running he still had no wider lead on them than that. Boyd and Asa Plank were not the kind to let the mere threat of a storm hold them back now. They were possessed of a dogged incentive, that would keep them going as long as he found the strength to lead them on.

Feeling the pressure, Gary straightened around again and kicked the buckskin forward. It obeyed reluctantly. He knew its legs were trembling under it with last, spent effort.

Nothing moved on the main street as they drifted through, with sheets of street dust whipping and stinging about the buckskin's legs. They passed a closed saloon, and another that seemed to be open but doing no business at this late hour. A signboard creaking over the dim-lit entrance of a hotel drew the briefest of glances; thought of shelter and a bed was almost an overpowering temptation, and yet Gary rode on. What he was looking for, anxiously, was a public livery or some such where he could find another mount to replace the buckskin that could carry him no farther.

He had reached the lower end of the street without success and was about to turn back when a flare of lightning showed him the words "NEVADA STAGES" painted across the front of a darkened building. Riding closer, he saw a battered coach parked in the weeds between the station and its adjoining barn. Beyond was the crisscross of corral poles. More lightning, and he caught a movement of horses in the pen.

A moment only, he hesitated. There was no sign of a night watchmen, no light showing. He sent his limping mount past the parked stage and into the shadows, and stepped tiredly down. He was so near exhaustion that his knees buckled and he had to catch at the saddlehorn to steady himself.

Being relay teams, these horses would undoubtedly be picked ones, sound of wind and limb even if not too familiar to a saddle. To take one in trade for the buckskin would be theft of a kind, he supposed, but Jim Gary was past worrying about that. He moved deliberately, stripping saddle and gear from the spent horse. The shuttering lightning was almost constant now. Brush and trees danced in the glare; thunder growled and bounced off the faces of the dark buildings.

He had his rope, and was stepping to unfasten the swing gate of the corral when the first hard, brief spatter of rain hit him.

Gary paused and stood listening to it pummel the hard earth, smelling the bitter dust it raised. The wind came stronger and as he grabbed at his hatbrim, cold blades seemed to probe deep at that spot of ache in his right breast where the puckered bullet scar was still fresh, not entirely healed. A sizzling fork of electricity fried the sky suddenly, and thunder rocked the ground as a horse in the corral bugled its terror.

Jim Gary said, "The hell with it!"

He coiled his rope and dropped it onto the saddle at his feet. Only the buckskin made him hesitate. He was about to set it loose with a slap on the rump, but it deserved better than that. The horse with the Swallowfork brand had carried him a lot of miles in this past week. Seeing its spent condition he had the stinging guilt of one who has used a faithful friend too severely. Meanwhile, he'd noticed a hay rick and the shine of a water trough in the corral. He slipped the fastenings of the gate long enough to turn the horse inside, and was a little moved at the eager way the lamed animal went limping over to feed and water.

The electric display had eased off abruptly, but the wind still pushed him, like a heavy hand, as he leaned to get his saddle. There was thick brush close by. He lugged the heavy stock rig into the midst of this and stowed it, making short work of that chore. Afterward, he retrieved his saddle roll and tossed it over a shoulder, and turned back toward the main street walking slantwise against the buffeting of rain-wet wind.

He had to cross the street to reach the hotel, and when he gained the other walk there was dust in his eyes and between his teeth. Beneath the swaying, creaking signboard he cleared his throat and spat, before walking into the sudden calm of the lobby.

The doors stood open, to let the cooling night wind enter. Light, here, was the dim glow of a turned-down oil lamp above the desk, that filled the corners with the clotted shadows of a lineup of cane rockers and heavy, sagging arm chairs. Gary carried his belongings over the worn linoleum to the desk and found the night man snoring behind it with head lolling against the wall. His long jaw had fallen open beneath a straggle of tobacco-stained mustache.

About to put out a hand and shake him awake, Jim Gary hesitated.

Keys hung from rows of nails on a board above the man's head. On an impulse he reached across and took one down at random and then, without disturbing the night clerk,

7

shouldered his roll again and turned toward the stairs. He climbed silently, through a muffled rolling of far-off thunder.

Another lamp laid streaky shadows along the upper hall. Gary searched briefly along the double row of closed doors and found the one his key fit. It turned out to be a forward room, above the street. He locked the door and crossed to the window beside the bed and ran it open to look out upon the night.

The sign creaked, a few yards distant. As he leaned there, with the wind blowing past him and cleaning out the stuffy airlessness of the room at his back, the rain began in earnest. His nostrils stung to the pungent smell of it soaking into dust-dry board.

There was a lamp on the washstand, with a few matches. Jim Gary lit up, revealing a room identical with a hundred such he'd slept in. He poured water into the basin and, stripping his shirt, rinsed the sweat and dirt from his upper body. He unhooked his shell belt and slung it over the bed's iron knob, drew and checked the gun and slid it under a pillow. Then, having blown the light, he dragged off his boots and stretched himself out. And in a matter of moments, with the wet wind blowing upon him through the window, Jim Gary slept.

He didn't know how long it was before he awoke. The night didn't feel much older. But some alert part of his brain had stood sentinel and, sorting out the noises of the darkness, now brought him warning. The wind had settled, stilling the constant squeal of the blowing signboard. Rain was a hushed and steady sound, and through it he heard others—the stomp of a hoof, a muttered exchange of talk. Instantly awake, Gary brought his gun from under the pillow and rolled over with it to the window.

Without moving from the bed, he could look straight down the hotel's clapboard front and see the motionless horsemen in the street below. They were two dim and shapeless figures, sheathed in wet rubber conchos that shone like metal through the sliding rain. He knew they were Boyd and Asa

8

Plank, caught up with him at last. He held his breath as he watched.

Where were the limits of human hatred and endurance? They must be fully as weary and discouraged as he was, and yet here they were, still in their saddles, still pressing after him. The trail was fresh and they knew it, even if this rain had come to wash out tracks. Now the two brothers were arguing, the cranky murmur of their voices rising louder still to Gary's window.

Boyd Plank, with the stolid stamina of two ordinary men, would want to keep going, no doubt; while Asa would be begging for a chance to rest, or perhaps even arguing that they ought to give this town a search before looking further. He could imagine Boyd's scornful answer: *Hell! The cowardly bastard is runnin' for his life. He knows we're close. He's out there somewhere ahead of us. And we got to get him before this storm washes out the last trace of his signs.*

Knowing the brothers, Jim Gary knew which would win the argument; Asa's keener intelligence giving way, as always, to the older man's assertive bigness. So he was not too greatly surprised when he saw them kick their horses forward and so drift away along the silent, shining wet street.

He stayed as he was, leaning in the open window to peer into the farther shadows for any movement while the handle of the sixgun ground into the stiffened fingers that clenched it. It wasn't the first time in this week that he'd found himself thinking sourly, *The hell with it! Let them find him, if they wanted to so badly!* Let the pair of them try their sorry, unskilled guns against his own.

But he pushed the thought away.

Only after an appreciable lapse of time could he let himself relax, and then by degrees. His pursuers had not shown themselves again, so he could only assume that they had passed him up. He stretched out again, therefore, with his hand on the hard surface of the gun. And finally, weary as he was, he let sleep come once more and claim him.

He awoke with sunlight full across him; he struggled to an

elbow and saw the town spread below his window and a morning sky swept almost clear of clouds. The mud of the street steamed under the sun. A horse and wagon creaked by; voices drifted in clean, washed air. Yonder, a man in a butcher's apron was sweeping down the walk before his place of business. He stopped in his work to nod greeting to a bonneted housewife.

Gary lay back again, still aware of a deep core of exhaustion even after a night's unbroken sleep. A fanwork of cracks ran across the ceiling plaster and he studied it a long time, and watched the trembling cloud of reflected light thrown on the wall by a puddle in the street below. He raised a hand, presently, passing it across the lean and muscled contours of his naked chest.

It was tender enough; he could feel the pull of new-healed tissues when he flexed his right arm and shoulder. But there was no sign of recurring fever. That was a distinct relief.

Jim Gary levered himself to his feet.

He had a razor in his belongings. As he shaved, taking his time, the life of this hotel came to him through flimsy walls— a door slamming, boots moving along the corridor and past his room, an occasional rumble of voices from somewhere. Once, downstairs he thought, a woman laughed and the sound had a musical quality that made his razor hold in mid-stroke while he looked at his own grave, gray eyes in the mirror, remembering something and wondering how many years it had been since he had heard a woman, a young woman, laugh in just that careless, charming way.

Perhaps because of the laugh, he was feeling old and used as he toweled and slipped into his shirt. The face that studied him in the glass, watching his lean hands do up the buttons of the shirt, was too finely drawn, all planes and angles and with nothing to soften the set of the mouth. It still showed the traces of his sickness. There was even a glint of gray at the temples of his straight, brown hair, but that was premature. He was, after all, only a year or so into his thirties. And his father had been a grizzled man, from the very earliest recollection of him.

With gun buckled on and hat in hand, he started to pick up his roll but then decided to leave it for the time being. He tossed it on the bed, walked from the room and locked the door behind him, afterward moving along the corridor toward the steps which led below.

The lobby was empty, and the night clerk's post deserted. But when Gary was still a half-dozen steps from the bottom of the stairs a door opened and a girl came out carrying an armload of clean and folded linens.

She went through the drop gate, around behind the desk, and had just set down her burden there when she happened to notice a stranger descending from the second story. Jim Gary saw the surprise that sprang into her glance and was a little amused. While she stood and stared at him, he moved casually down the remaining steps and traveled the worn linoleum to the desk. From his pocket he took his room key and two silver dollars, and laid them in front of her. He said, pleasantly, "That be enough for the room?"

Blue eyes widened, then frowned as she looked down at the money and the key. She was not a tall girl. What he mainly saw was the top of her head—the part, like a ruled white line, and dark hair falling away in soft curls behind small and well-shaped ears. There was a clean smell about her, like that of the linens on the counter at her elbow.

Gary saw her glance stray to the book lying open on the desk. He said, "You won't find me in the register."

She looked up quickly. She was groping for words, plainly puzzled and maybe even a little afraid of him. But when she found her voice, she was completely businesslike. "The charge is three dollars."

He fished up another, and she took it in silence. He liked the way she moved; he liked her voice, and it occurred to him that hers must have been the laughter he'd heard, the sound that reminded him of things so long ago as to be almost forgotten. Now she asked, in the same tone of bafflement, "Do you mean to stay long?"

"No. I'll be leaving. There are some things in the room," he went on. "I'll pick them up later, if it's all right." She only nodded.

Beyond the desk, through a curtained archway, Gary had glimpsed the checkered tablecloths and cane-seated chairs of a small dining room. "Serving breakfast?"

"For the next hour," she told him.

"Thanks." Jim Gary nodded, and walked out of the hotel.

As he drew his hat on and settled it, he reflected with a narrow smile that you really couldn't expect to make a sudden appearance in a place like this, dropping out of nowhere—out of the sky, practically—and not cause some kind of reaction. But he shrugged the thought aside, because there were more urgent things to occupy him.

This town and its people were no concern of his. What he had to do first of all was find out for sure whether Boyd and Asa Plank were here, or had actually ridden through.

II

THE town was Antler, Nevada. He learned that much from signs on business houses up and down the crooked street. As a town there was hardly anything to distinguish it. He walked along a street that was drying out after the night's storm, and he found himself watching doorways and the openings between buildings and wondering if the Planks would go so far as to lay an ambush. It didn't sound like them, but you couldn't be sure, given their motivation and their fear of his gun.

So he cruised the town warily, and a tired impatience began to take hold of him. But he reached the lower end without incident and so turned back, ready now to believe his precautions weren't necessary, that his pursuers had gone on last night.

A coach and six had just come in over the south road and was standing at the station, with the horses blowing and stomping in the harness. Jim Gary stopped a moment, just across the way, to watch driver and passengers alighting while a hostler hurried out to see to the teams. He was minded of the buckskin he'd left in the corral, and of the saddle hidden in the bushes at the back of the lot. And then, as a sudden thought suggested itself to him, he turned on impulse and moved across the puddled road to where a balding man, wearing steel-rimmed spectacles and sleeve supporters, was at work unbuckling the leather shield of the rear boot. He asked this person, "When does the next stage leave?"

The man peered at him. "Stage for where?"

It hardly mattered. Gary said as much, and saw the faintly suspicious look that he got through the flashing spectacles. But the station agent only shrugged. "This here is the one that goes south twice a week, to connect with the railroad. Won't be rolling again till day after tomorrow. Only other coach we schedule is a weekly feeder stage to Cooper Hill.

13

That old mudwagon yonder," he added, and jerked his head toward the battered vehicle that stood starkly in the barren yard between station and barn. "It pulls out at six tonight."

"Copper Hill?" Jim Gary repeated. "Where's that?"

"Mining camp, in the hills thirty miles east. Ain't surprising you mightn't have heard of it, especially if you're a stranger. It's been pretty dead. But they're reopening one of the old mines and things are startin' to boom again. Were you lookin' for work?" the man asked suddenly.

"Maybe," Gary lied. Let him think so.

"Well, everything's cattle, here around Antler. Now, if it's Copper Hill you're interested in—" The station agent interrupted himself, looking past Gary at someone who was just stepping down from the coach. "Here's the man you should talk to! Webb Toland. He's the one is gonna have that camp back on the map by time he's finished." And before Jim Gary could stop him, the other was calling out, "Mr. Toland! Feller here is looking for a job over at your camp."

Gary turned, a little impatiently. He was a lean, well-dressed man who ran a glance over the stranger's trailworn clothing. Webb Toland said dubiously, "You don't have the look of a singlejack man."

"I suppose not," he agreed indifferently.

But the other's glance had stopped, suddenly, on the gun strapped to Gary's waist. It lingered there a long moment, and then slowly the eyes lifted to his face. And despite himself Jim Gary experienced a slight but distinct thrill of shock.

It was the eyes that did it. In a darkly handsome, almost swarthy face, they were pale and seemingly suffused by a kind of tawny glow. Gary was minded of the eyes of a mountain cat that had come close one night to investigate his campfire.

Toland came just about to an even height with him, but Gary felt he probably edged the man by a good ten pounds. There was indeed something feline in this slim, dark man— poised litheness; some quality that suggested Webb Toland was a man you would not forget.

14

"I didn't catch the name," Toland said suggestively.

A moment only Gary hesitated. Then he told it, curious to see if the name would strike any spark of recognition in those watching yellow eyes. He couldn't say for sure whether it did or not; the eyes revealed no more than they wanted to. But whether it was the name or the gun, something in Gary had struck an interest in this man from Copper Hill.

"I just don't know," Toland was saying slowly. "I couldn't guarantee anything. But you might look me up at the Copper Queen. I'll be keeping you in mind." Gary had a definite feeling that the other was really considering him, that there was some purpose behind his words for which he could perhaps want a man like the stranger, and a gun like his with its look of frequent use.

"All right," said Gary. "Thanks."

And that ended it. Toland turned away to hail the station man who had just returned to the coach for an armload of stuff from the trunk. "I checked a bag through, Johnson. See that it gets on the other coach and send it up tonight. I'll be leaving right away."

"Sure thing," the man promised. A last stab of the tawny eyes thrust at Gary, as though to place him firmly in mind. Then Webb Toland heeled around and strode away, into the town. Johnson turned to the stranger. "Any luck with him?" he asked.

"Could be."

Johnson nodded sagely. "Toland's a damn big man. He's doin' big things at the Queen. He's ready to put her back in production, now, usin' some newfangled method or other that nobody'd heard of back in the days of the first boom. You get in good with him, mister, and you're fixed."

Jim Gary nodded absently, for he had no real interest in what this Webb Toland was doing at the mining camp. He had learned all he wanted, and already knew his next step, the stage to Copper Hill had supplied the answer.

He was starting to walk away when a passerby happened

to remark to the station agent: "Did the sheriff have any ideas to offer about them three Swallowfork broncs?"

"Hell, no!" Johnson answered as Gary halted, instantly alert. "George Ruby's as much in the dark as I am. No tracks left, after the rain last night. No way of knowin' how they got into the open, or what happened to the horses that were taken in exchange."

"Well, what's he aimin' to do about it?"

"Somebody better do something!" Johnson promised in a dark tone. "The stage company won't cotton to first-grade stock bein' sneaked out of its corral! I figure it'll take a vet and a month of feeding to bring them run-down nags they traded me back into any kind of shape!"

Gary had heard enough. He moved on up the sidewalk, his expressionless face showing nothing. *Three* Swallowforks! Now, what—All at once he understood: Boyd and Asa Plank, their fagged horses stumbling under them as they followed him into town last night, must have figured exactly the same as the man they were pursuing. They'd gone looking for a trade of horses, and found the stageline corral. And if so, they'd undoubtedly seen the buckskin and guessed that Jim Gary had a fresh mount under him. And so they'd been tolled ahead, and by this morning would probably be miles down the south trail.

His spirits rose perceptibly. Sooner or later, of course, his pursuers would know that they'd been tricked, and they'd backtrack then. But he was assured now of a margin of time, to accomplish what he had planned to throw them off the trail for good.

With the pressures suddenly lifted, he realized that he was ravenously hungry. He turned back into the town, ready now to discover what kind of breakfast they served at that hotel.

He saw the girl again, the moment he stepped into the lobby. She was behind the desk, talking to a fat man and another he recognized as the clerk who'd been asleep at his post last night. They all three halted their conversation and looked at Jim Gary as he entered, and they did it in a way that told him he was under discussion. He put his glance directly on the girl, held it until he saw her color slightly and break gaze, biting at her lower lip. He ignored the two men with her, and went on through the lobby and ducked the low arch into the dining room.

He seemed to be the last for breakfast. He chose a table that gave him a view of the lobby door, with an open window at his elbow, and gave his order of eggs and bacon and fried potatoes to the woman who came from the kitchen to take it. As he waited, he sat and frowned at the drab scene framed in the window and realized again how bone-tired he still was.

The bullet wound, the lung fever that had resulted from it, and now these days of trailing—it would be a long time, he supposed, before he had completely overcome the effects of them.

His food arrived from the kitchen, and he had barely started on it when the fat man he'd seen in the lobby came through the archway, looked around, and then walked directly to Gary's table and pulled back a chair for himself. It groaned as he settled his weight in it. The front of his coat fell back and gave Jim Gary a look at the piece of metal pinned to the man's shirt pocket.

The sheriff said, in a rough voice, "You're the man Tracy was tellin' me about. Tracy Bannister," he explained impatiently, when the name drew no sign of recognition. He jerked his big head toward the lobby door behind him. "She owns this hotel. I'm George Ruby," he went on, shifting back onto the hind legs of the chair. "I got some questions to ask you. First off, I think you might tell me your name."

Gary had decided already that he didn't like this man. He didn't like the faintly sweating face, the faintly bulging black eyes. And he didn't like the man's blunt approach. Remembering Webb Toland's apparent failure to identify him, he shrugged and forked another piece of bacon before he answered briefly, "I doubt that the name matters. You've probably never heard it."

Color was stung into the fat man's cheeks. His head jerked and he brought his chair forward, and laid one wide hand on the table top. "Don't get smart with me!" But he settled again as he met the look the other gave him. He frowned, and ran a fleshy fist across his mouth. "Let's start all over again," he said roughly. "If I was you, I'd answer the questions!"

"Any reason I should? You've got nothing on me."

"No? How about this?" Ruby continued. "It was pretty damned peculiar, you walkin' in here last night without a word to anybody, and helping yourself to a key and a room."

"This morning," Jim Gary reminded him, "Miss Bannister was offered payment for the room and she accepted it. So you can't make anything of that!" Calmly he drank from his coffee cup, set it down. "Want to try again, Sheriff?"

George Ruby scowled into the stranger's eyes. "All right! A couple of horses was took out of the stage company's corral last night, and three worn-out broncs left in their place. I'm thinkin' you must have rode one of them Swallowforks into this town."

"If that's a crime, then you'll have to prove it on me."

"Damn it, you didn't just drop out of nowhere!" The sheriff checked his flare-up of temper. For a moment he said nothing, as though waiting for Gary to speak, but the latter was methodically finishing his plate, and after a moment Ruby took the thing up again. His voice had lowered again to its former rumble.

"I've been tryin' to think where I'd heard of that Swallowfork brand, and it seems to me now I remember. It's a northern outfit. If I ain't mistaken, it's located somewhere up around Mogul Valley, where they been havin' 'em a range war. I know the kind of riffraff always collects for a thing like that! Hired toughs, and gunhands! Now that the fightin' around Mogul has come to a windup, wouldn't surprise me if some of them hired guns should start drifting down this

way. And looks to me that's exactly what's happening!" He
added pointedly, "Who rode them two other broncs?"

Gary said, with a shrug, "You're telling this yarn." He
drained the last of his coffee, pushed the wreckage of his
meal aside.

"I see you pack a gun," the sheriff said coldly. "You pack it
like it was for more than show. I'm telling you now, we don't
need your kind! We got our troubles—the makings of a little
range war of our own, right here at Antler. Now, maybe you
knew that; maybe somebody even sent up to Mogul Valley,
to fetch you. If they did—I'm tellin' you to forget it! And it's
the law giving your orders!"

Very deliberately, Jim Gary pushed back his chair. He
told himself it was foolish to let this man anger him, but such
was his mood and he was too tired to fight it. He got to his
feet and, looking down at the sheriff, he said, "You're taking
a lot for granted. I admit nothing, and that goes for Mogul
Valley and for those horses you say you found. Far as you're
concerned, I'm still the man that dropped in from nowhere.
Take my advice and don't try to make anything more out of
it. As for me, I intend to leave when I'm good and ready!"

He left George Ruby sitting there, and walked back into
the lobby. The girl was behind the desk, sorting mail that
had come in on the morning stage. She lifted a startled look
that she tried to disguise, as she saw the stranger come
toward her.

"My key, please," he said.

Tracy Bannister considered the request, her blue eyes
searching his. Then very deliberately, and with no move
toward the rack of keys, she turned the registration book
around and shoved the pen in its holder toward him, and
waited.

Jim Gary had to smile a little, amused at the curiosity he
had unintentionally roused in these people. The girl, at least,
was direct about it, so to satisfy her he took the pen and
calmly signed his name. Not answering his cool smile, she

very soberly took his key off the rack and he accepted it with a nod of thanks.

When he started for the stairs, he knew she stood and watched him out of sight.

Later, in his room, he stretched out on the bed again and felt weariness pour through him. It was stored up in some deeper well of his being, apparently, than he had realized. Completely relaxed, he let it have its way with him while he thought with a new confidence of the road ahead.

The stage for Copper Hill left at six o'clock. That would serve. Sooner or later, Boyd and Asa Plank would be retracing their course. When they reached Antler they would quickly pick up the trail again, but not soon enough to do them any good. At the mining camp he would get himself a horse and push on east through the hills, able now to take his time and bury his tracks so thoroughly that there could be no hope of finding them. Eventually even those two would have to give up the hunt, and thus he'd be freed at last of everything connected with that grim business at Mogul Valley.

Everything, but the constant reminder of a new-healed wound in his chest. . . .

Six o'clock, he thought, and the whole day till then his own. With the long tensions lifted, the need for rest which had been only partly satisfied last night rose again, stronger now and not to be denied. He set his mental clock to rouse him, and was content to let conscious thought slip away.

III

It was something in the corridor that woke him this time. He lay a moment, bringing dulled senses into focus, coming out of a sleep so deep that he wasn't even sure for a moment where he was; the past week might never have happened. Then he remembered, in a rush, and at the same moment, recognized the sounds that had roused him: Uncertain footsteps, a noise as of something sliding along the wall beyond his door, an anxious whispering. Then he heard a man's deep groan, and it was this that brought him off the bed.

His gun was in his hand as he padded in stockinged feet to the door and threw it open. For a moment, he could only stare.

Two people were in the hallway—the girl, Tracy, and a big, black-bearded man who looked to be nearly twice her size. She had an arm about his waist and was trying to support his weight but it was plainly too much for her. He sagged heavily against her and against the wall. Gary saw the blood, then, that had nearly drenched the whole left side of the man's hickory shirt.

For a moment they held that tableau, with the girl returning his stare. She looked wide-eyed and frightened, and almost crushed by the blind weight she was trying to support with her own slight frame. But as Jim Gary started to her aid she shook her head and frantically whispered, "No! Don't come near him!"

Then the bearded man went slack and, knees buckling, began to slide down the wall, bearing her with him. Gary didn't hesitate. He stepped forward, shoving his gun behind his waistband, and took hold of the hurt man. He was something of a burden, even for Jim Gary. He thrust a shoulder beneath the other's armpit and got the limp weight settled, afterward saying to the girl, "What do you want done with him?"

Tracy Bannister had a key in her hand, but she seemed to

have forgotten it. She only looked at Gary, and shook her head again with pale lips open on an unspoken protest. And he, waiting, turned impatient. "You want him to bleed to death?" he suggested harshly.

"No. No, of course not!" That had jarred her loose. She turned and hastened to a door across from his own and fumbled the key into the lock. As the door swung open, Gary brushed past her with his burden. "On the bed," she whispered, and moved hastily to draw back the spread. Gary eased him down, lifted the booted legs one after the other, and got him straightened out. The man lay with eyes half closed and the breath sawing in his chest, obviously not more than half conscious. His blood was already staining the sheets.

The girl seemed unaware or indifferent to the ruin of her high-necked shirtwaist. She turned to Gary, hands twisting and knotting and a deep anxiety in her eyes. "You must forget that you saw him!" she whispered. "You must forget what's happened here. Promise me!"

He frowned. "Of course. But can't I help you with him?"

"No!" she answered quickly. "No, I can do everything. Just go away! Please!"

Gary considered her for a moment, and then shrugged. "All right," he said a little stiffly. "If that's how you want it!"

She was a capable person but hardly, he thought, the one for a job like this. Still, she'd refused his help and there was nothing more he could do. He was through the door and had it almost closed behind him when a sudden anguished outburst from Tracy Bannister halted him.

"Wait. . . ."

Turning back, he saw from her look that she was torn between conflicting emotions—her uncertainty about him, and her need for help. "If you will . . .?"

"Name it."

"Down in back of the hotel—his horse. It mustn't be found here. Get rid of it; it doesn't matter how."

He nodded. "All right."

"And I forgot to thank you, Mr. Gary."

Jim Gary considered her for a moment, his total puzzlement over all this tempered by a concern he couldn't help feeling for the girl. She was frightened, pathetically alone in this unnamed emergency. Her eyes were a dark stain against the pallor of her face, and he saw her hand tremble on the bedpost.

He said again, "All right," and left her, carefully closing the door.

He returned briefly to his own room for his boots and gunbelt, and then went quickly down through the silent building. The lobby was empty. He found the door to the rear hall and went past the kitchen and out through a screen door into the weedy lot in back of the hotel. Barrels and empty boxes were stacked against the building's blank rear wall. In the skimpy shade of a poplar tree, a saddled horse stood on trailing reins and cropped at the rank weeds.

It was a spotted gray, a gelding, and a big one, such as anyone the size of the hurt man would need to carry his weight. The heavy stock saddle identified the animal, for it was smeared and slippery with blood. Hard to say how far it had brought its wounded rider, but Gary would judge it had been for some considerable distance. The gray was upset and jumpy. It edged away as he moved toward it and he saw the Spur branded on its shoulder. He spoke to settle the animal, and got the reins.

Tracy Bannister had said merely to get rid of it, prevent it from being found where it was. He had no better idea, so he simply knotted the split leathers and hooked them over the blood-smeared horn, and then gave the gelding's rump a slap. It leaped under his hand like a frightened cat, snorting and shaking its head. Gary scooped up a couple of stones but they weren't needed. The gray had already settled into a trot. He watched it move off into the sage that stretched behind the town, its empty stirrups flopping. When it dropped from sight across a dip of the ground he threw his pebbles aside and turned back to the hotel.

His hand was on the screen when something made him pause and look behind him.

It was not a sound, merely the feeling one sometimes gets of being watched. He stood there in the sun and made a careful survey, his hand drawn near his gun, but he saw no one. Still, there were the windows and the doors and the corners of neighboring buildings where an observer could have seen him driving the horse away and then ducked out of sight to keep from being noticed. Gary scowled, bothered by this thought, but though he waited for a moment there was no sound or movement to confirm that momentary suspicion. He shook his head, and walked back inside.

At the door of the room where he had left Tracy Bannister he started to knock and then held it, remembering his dismissal a moment ago; perhaps she would rather he left her alone. But as he hesitated, there was a sudden burst of incoherent speech, in a man's deep voice, and the girl's quick cry of alarm. He dropped his hand on the knob, then, and pushed the door open.

The hurt man was trying to get up from the bed, and meaningless sounds spilled from his bearded lips as Tracy struggled with him to hold him down. Gary saw the situation and, quickly shutting the door, strode forward to help. Out of his head with pain, eyes wild and unseeing, the man on the bed had a frenzied strength that was enough even for Gary to cope with.

But he held him down, avoiding the thrashing of the booted legs, and suddenly the fight ran out of the other and let him drop back limp. Gary straightened to look at the girl. What he saw in her face settled his mind. He said, "I'll do this," and there was not strength in her to object.

She had managed to tear away the blood-soaked shirt sleeve, to reveal the wound—a clean one, a rifle shot he judged, that had drilled the man's left shoulder and gone on through without crippling damage. The flow of blood had been heavy but the worst of that seemed ended. Gary started to say, "You got any—" but the girl was already offering him the materials that she must have had in a pocket of her skirt. There was a bottle of liniment, a quantity of clean cloth. He took the bottle, saying, "Tear me some strips." It would do her good to have something to turn her hand to.

The liniment was powerful stuff that he could scarcely have brought himself to pour into a raw wound if the man had been conscious. Even as it was the big head twisted on the pillow and a groan broke from the bearded lips as the fiery stuff bit deep into damaged tissues.

The girl had the bandages ready now and Gary placed compresses over both ends of the bullet hole and then wrapped the shoulder tightly. "That's as good as we can do," he said gruffly, and straightened. Turning to the girl, he surprised a look on her white face that alarmed him into moving to put a hand on her arm.

She was trembling; she ran a hand shakily across her forehead and murmured, "I'm . . . all right!"

"You'd better sit down!"

She tried to protest, but he led her to a cane rocker and she seemed willing enough to drop into it. Gary went to the washstand and poured a glass of water from the big china pitcher, and brought it to her.

She drank, and shook her head in disgust at her own behavior. Her color was better now, and he decided she wasn't going to faint. She said, "I'm sorry! It's silly to let the sight of a little blood—"

"Had you ever tried to work on a gunshot wound before?" he demanded.

"No."

"Then there's nothing silly about it!" He took the glass and returned it to the commode. He leaned there, folding his arms and frowning at the girl in the chair. On the bed, the hurt man lay sleeping, his deep chest rising and falling steadily. Gary indicated him.

"Wasn't there anyone else? A doctor he could have gone to?"

"And have the word get out?" she countered. "Have his enemies learn that he's lying wounded and helpless? There's no telling what they would do if they had this chance!"

Gary frowned. "Who is he?"

"You saw the brand on his horse," she reminded him dryly.

"The Spur? That wouldn't mean anything to me." And then, seeing the complete disbelief that came into her face, he said impatiently and in a sharper voice, "Look! You and the sheriff appear to have the same notion, and you're wrong! I know nothing at all about this country. Nobody sent for me, neither him"— he nodded toward the bed—"nor his enemies, whoever they are! You can believe that, Miss Bannister."

"Can I?"

She came out of the chair, and walked over to stand before him where she could look directly into his eyes. Her own were skeptical and troubled, as they tried to read the riddle of this man. "How do I know what to believe about you, Jim Gary? When you just suddenly appear out of nowhere with no way for anyone to tell who you are, where you came from?"

He answered her look with a level regard. "As far as you're concerned, it doesn't need to matter who I am! I assure you I didn't mean anything by the way I walked into your place last night and helped myself to a room. But I had a reason for doing it."

He saw her eyes widen as enlightenment came to her. Her voice sounded a little breathless, shaken at what she had all at once guessed. "There's someone after you! That's it, isn't it?" She added, almost in a whisper, "The law?"

"You're pretty close. But it isn't the law." Gary straightened from his leaning position, letting his arms drop to his sides. His fingers brushed the handle of the holstered gun and the reminder turned his manner brusque.

"I'll be in town only a few hours, and then I'm leaving. Meanwhile I've got no concern with anything that might be going on here. Certainly, I have no reason to do him any harm." He indicated the wounded man.

"Then you *will* forget you saw him? You won't let a word

slip to anybody. Anyone at all? You'll give me your promise?"
"You've already got it."

"Thank you," she said, and he knew then that she had lost her doubt of him. He was as much a mystery to her as ever, but Tracy Bannister must have decided with some obscure woman's knowledge that this was a man she would believe and trust.

Jim Gary, for his part, looked at this girl and he felt a stirring of impulses and regrets that were strange to him. In the world in which he moved, women were the unattractive creatures of cowtown bars and dancehalls; or they were ranchers' wives, drawn out and brutalized by their hard and inescapable existence. He didn't know when he had encountered youth and real physical attraction. Tracy Bannister he judged to be in her early twenties; even the drudgery of trying to manage a hotel in a backward prairie village hadn't yet killed the freshness of girlhood in her, or dulled the color of her cheeks.

He supposed it would happen to her, too, even though there was something about her that suggested here was one who would, at least, manage to escape from that fate by one means or another. But in any event it was nothing that could concern him. There was no place for any woman in his life. Nor would she have a second glance for him if she knew the truth about him and the uses to which his gun was put.

So he put these reflections from his mind and asked "If there's anything more I can do, you'll let me know?"

"I will," she promised, and a smile took the last traces of shock from her face. "You've been more than kind."

Jim Gary walked out of the room, leaving her there. And found a man standing in the gloomy hallway with a drawn gun in his hand.

The meeting was a total surprise to both of them. The man had been looking with close and intent interest at a dark spot on the wallpaper. At the sound of the door opening his head jerked and the gun tipped up, the inch or two it took to bring it full on the other man. Gary, for his part, had begun a move toward his own holster that was almost a reflex action. He quickly checked it.

So the two stood and looked at each other, that gun leveled squarely. Silhouetted against the dim glow of a window at the far end of the hall, the man was an oddly misshapen figure, with one shoulder hitched higher than the other and his head held stiffly as though on the end of a rod stuck into his body. Gary could make out little of his face except the eyes, the whites of them dusky, and a heavy brush of dark mustache. But he remembered suddenly the uneasy impression he'd felt, during those moments in back of the hotel, that curious and unseen eyes were watching everything he did.

He saw now what it was this stranger had been studying with such interest. On the wall, where the wounded man had leaned his weight while Tracy Bannister supported him, there was a dark smear of blood.

The man with the gun looked past Gary at the closed door and he demanded, in a hoarse voice, "Is that where you've got him?"

"Got who?" retorted Gary, letting his hand hang free of the holster. He had a feeling that if he touched it, that other gun would go off.

"Matt Winship!" the man answered loudly. "Don't try to stall me! I seen you chase that gray of his away from here. It ain't all I seen, either—blood, on the saddle! I even rode after and caught the damn bronc, just to make sure. The old devil's been shot, ain't he? Shot bad, I'd judge," he added, indicating the bloodstain on the wall beside him. "Now, where is he?"

Tracy's frightened warning about Winship's enemies came back to him, and now he began to understand it. He said coldly, "Why do you want to know? So you can finish the job while he's laid up and defenseless?"

The man didn't even trouble to deny it. His interest had focused on the stranger who faced him now, and he said, "I guess you must be this gent the whole town is wonderin' about. Gary, somebody read it on the book downstairs. Just what's your game, mister? Where do you figure in this?"

"Put your gun away and walk out of here, or you may find out!"

The head jerked on its mismated shoulders. A sound like a snarl broke from the other. "A bad *hombre*, huh? Don't try anything with me, Mr. Gary! Stand aside and let me see what's in that room."

"I'll say it again," Jim Gary warned without raising his voice. "Be careful what you try!"

For a moment, the tableau held as the man measured the warning and Gary waited to see what he would do. Even with a gun leveled against him, there was something in the stranger's apparent lack of fear that seemed to hold this other one back. Gary sensed the hesitation, and something of his respect for the potential danger in the man began to fall away. Yet even a coward can be dangerous with a drawn gun in his hand.

And then the door behind Gary opened and he heard Tracy Bannister's gasp of alarm. It brought the man's stare whipping to her. For an instant no one moved, or spoke. The heavy mustache lifted, above a crooked and humorless grin that showed the gleam of white teeth. The man said, heavily, "Well, Tracy! Just what kind of room service do you give your guests?"

Gary hit him.

He did it almost without thinking, despite the gun. He made a sharp step forward and the edge of his left hand struck the other's arm while he drove a short and jolting right against his jaw. Taken wholly by surprise, the man was slammed back against the wall and the gun jumped out of his fingers. It hit the toe of his boot and slid away, and he stood there as though dazed with the unexpectedness of the blow.

"What's his name?" Jim Gary asked the girl.

"Vince Alcord."

"All right, Alcord. Let's hear you apologize!"

At this command, the other rallied a little. "To her?" he cried, in a tone of harsh bluster. "Like hell I will! She ain't foolin' anybody. The whole country's known for a long time how it was between her and that old goat of a Winship!"

The back of Gary's hand cut him sharply across the mouth; blood spurted and Alcord's head was jarred sharply against the wall. Speech broken off, he stared, blinded with pain, and the blood began a slow trickle down his chin.

"Let him go!" cried Tracy Bannister. She caught at Gary's sleeve, to prevent him hitting the man again. Her voice sounded muffled with anxiety and shame. "Please! I don't care. . . ."

But Jim Gary jerked free, and now his own gun slid into his hand and it leveled on the other man's lean middle. His voice trembled with real anger. "Walk down the stairs and out of here!"

Vince Alcord looked back at him from eyes hot with fury. His tongue snaked out and touched the lip Gary's blow had split. At the taste of his own blood he shuddered and his chest heaved to a sobbing breath. But with the advantage of a drawn gun shifted now, he could see that the choice wasn't his. His mouth worked on unspoken words. And then he jerked about and started toward the stair well.

Following, Jim Gary saw the gun Alcord had dropped and paused long enough to scoop it up, exchanging it for his own weapon which he returned to its holster. Stair treads creaked under the solid tramp of boots, as the two men dropped down to the deserted lobby. They crossed the room, Jim Gary herding Alcord at the point of his own gun, to the propped-open doors. But there, at last, the man balked. He half turned, and his voice held a tight trembling.

"This ain't the last you'll hear from me," he began. "You nor that trollop upstairs."

Gary trusted himself to spend no more words on him. He was in a sour mood, and newly-healed muscles ached with the savage blows he'd thrown at Alcord. He merely placed the flat of a hand against the man's shoulder, spun him around again with a shove that propelled him sharply through the doorway. Vince Alcord lost balance and in trying to re-

30

gain it caught the tilted heel of one boot over the edge of the sidewalk planking. He let out a squawk as he went down, to land belly-flat in the street's drying mud.

Standing in the door, Gary watched him scramble. Alcord had lost his hat. He got one knee and a propping hand under him and hunched there panting, black hair streaming into his face as he stared wildly at this stranger. He said, in a voice that was a choked yell, "Mister, if I had my gun—"

Gary looked at the weapon he held. With an indifferent shrug, he tossed it out to the man, and it made a couple of flat spins before it struck the dirt a few inches from Alcord's hand. He watched the man eye it, then lift his stare again to where Gary waited with his gun arm hanging idly alongside his own holstered sixgun. It was up to him, now, and suddenly Alcord wasn't so sure. He hesitated, making no move.

"Pick it up," Gary ordered in tired disgust. "Pick it up and put it in your holster or use it! Whichever one you want!"

"Another time, maybe." The man was making an effort to maintain a certain bluster, but he couldn't hide the clear fact that he was defeated, backing water. He spat blood from his mashed lip, and grabbed up his hat and dragged it on after shaking the hair back from his sweating face. On his feet, he looked for a long moment at the gun. He leaned and picked it up then, carefully, so that the watching Gary should not mistake his intentions. He shoved it deep into its holster.

"Another time," he repeated harshly, with a thrust of his glance at the unmoving figure in the hotel entrance. And then he swung his mismatched shoulders and turned away, striding toward a rawboned black that stood tied to a nearby rack. He jerked the reins free and lifted himself into the saddle. He pulled the bronc's head around and jabbed the spurs so savagely that the bay reared and came down in a lunging run.

Vince Alcord didn't look back. He put the black along the street and went off at a hard lope, one shod hoof striking up

THE LURKING GUN

a fountain of muddy water from a gathered puddle. He looked like a man with an intent and serious purpose.

But Jim Gary didn't watch him out of sight. He was searching the street quickly to discover how many witnesses there had been to the scene. The sidewalks were deserted but he had already noted a couple of riders who, in passing, had drawn a hasty rein as Alcord came plummeting out of the doorway and into the street mud, almost under the noses of their horses. They were still sitting there, and now Gary looked at them more closely.

As a range-bred man will do, he glanced at the horses first and saw that they were good ones; he caught the Spur brands on them. And then he lifted his cool stare toward the riders of these Winship mounts. The man was young, a handsome and clean-shaven type with yellow sideburns and a spoiled and quarrelsome look in the blue eyes that scowled at Gary; a man who dressed in whipcord breeches and a silk shirt and boots that carried a high and unscuffed polish. But you wouldn't be apt to notice the man, after a first cursory examination, if your eyes happened then to touch upon his companion.

She was a beauty, a redhead with the milky complexion that sometimes goes with hair of that particular deep, rich color. She rode sidesaddle, in a green skirt that hung long over the rounded fullness of hip and thigh, and she carried that handsome head of hers with an erect proudness: her shoulders straight, her bosom swelling in her open-throated blouse, a riding crop across her knees. She looked down from the back of her horse, with a direct and interested stare, meeting Gary's look directly. And he saw her companion turn in the saddle and say something to the woman, his scowl petulant and showing anger.

Gary had no way of knowing their names, but from the Spur brand on their horses he judged they must own some connection with the hurt man on the bed in that room upstairs. Certainly, if they were kin of Matt Winships they would be concerned to know of what had happened to him.

32

But an obscure impulse kept him silent. Tracy Bannister had said not to let a word slip to anybody. And so, understanding exactly nothing of what he had found himself involved in here, he decided to take her literally.

He turned his back on that handsome pair of riders, walked back inside the building and slowly up the lobby stairs, favoring the slow ache in his hurt right side.

IV

PAUL KEATING pulled his attention away from that door where the man had vanished, and turned to his wife. She was still staring after the stranger, with an expression that put a cold and clotted tightness inside him and, for the moment, completely knocked from his mind whatever he had been about to say.

He was by nature a jealous man and he knew it, a man completely insecure in his relation with his handsome wife. Even now, even under the pressure of an anxiety that was like a steam gauge on the point of blowing, he could feel this other, crawling emotion of a sick resentment that was always there ready to rise in him at any provocation.

Fern spoke, and her words were enough to make his hand tighten on the reins and bulge the tight muscle along the line of his jaw. "I wonder who he is?"

Keating said, without being able to hold the curt tension from his voice, "Does it matter?"

"It would be interesting to know. You saw how he handled Vince Alcord like a child. Spur could use a few men like that!"

She looked at her husband as she spoke, a tilted glance of her long-lashed and beautiful eyes. He had, as he so often did, the feeling that she was amused and deliberately taunting him, and at this time and place the idea was beyond bearing. His scowl deepened. He said, "Come along!" and jabbed his horse forward with the spur.

A few yards farther on, his wife caught up with him. Reading his mood, Fern crowded her mare against his horse and brought it to a stand, beneath the arching shadow of a cottonwood that had littered the sidewalk and street with branches thrown down in last night's storm. She reached and laid a firm hand upon his coatsleeve, and her voice was stern and vibrant.

"Paul! Remember! Whatever happens, whatever we find,

34

you've got to act like yourself. Do you understand me? You must manage to be calm and face this through!"

"How can I?" he groaned, and swung his head. "I tell you, the old man was looking right at me when I pulled the trigger. I know he saw me!"

"Surely the distance would have been too great! Be a man, Paul, for God's sake!"

He lifted a flaring look at her. "You can say that! If it weren't for you, and that crook Toland—"

"Are you blaming *me*, now?" She met him with a look as hot as his own. "Did I tell you to do it?"

She felt the muscles of his forearm pull taut and, seeing the shifting of his glance, swung around as George Ruby came toward them through the dappled shade that the big tree cast along the sidewalk plankings. The sheriff gave them a preoccupied look; then he reacted to the woman's beauty. "Afternoon, Miz Keating," he said, smiling toothily as he touched hatbrim. He nodded in passing to her husband. If he noticed anything odd in their unanswering silence he gave no sign, but strode on with his ponderous tread. Fern's hand tightened on her husband's arm and she leaned closer, whispering fiercely.

"You see? The sheriff knows nothing. He doesn't even know that Matt's been hurt!"

Paul Keating shook his head, bewildered. "But where could the old man have got to, if he didn't reach town? I tell you, the last I saw his horse was pointed directly this way!"

"Then it's obvious he didn't make it. He got off the trail somewhere and is probably lying dead."

"I hope he is!" the man said hoarsely, and his clenched fist struck the pommel of his saddle. "Oh, God, how I hope so! I didn't want to kill him, but I had no choice. I couldn't let him see those books; I couldn't have him finding out."

"Be quiet, can't you?" Her fierce whisper silenced him, as his voice began to rise out of control. There was no one in earshot but she looked with apprehension at a wagon and team jouncing toward them over the ruts. "Do you want the

35

whole town hearing? Now, listen to me," she went on as the man subsided under the warning. "There's still one possibility. If Matt did get as far as town, he might have gone directly to the doctor's place and the sheriff wouldn't necessarily have heard yet. We've got to ride around there and find out."

"To the doctor's house?" Looking at her, Paul Keating's face was gray with sickness. Cold sweat made a sheen across the planes of his cheeks. "And supposing he's there? How do you think I can bear to look him in the face, wondering what he knows?"

"Bluff it through."

"I can't!"

She must have seen, then, that he spoke the sober truth. She gave the thing up with a sigh and a grimace dropping her hand away from his arm. "All right," she said coldly. "I'll go alone, then. Wait for me at Laurie Pitkin's. I'll come as soon as I know anything."

Not delaying for an answer, she used her riding crop and the fine bay mare spurted ahead. Keating watched her turn into the street where the doctor's house stood, and vanish. He shook himself, as though to bring himself out of a trance of terror that had locked his muscles. He brought a handkerchief from his pocket and wiped his face with it and his hand was trembling as he stuffed the cloth away again.

He knew what he needed; he could feel the burning thirst for it at the back of his throat, suddenly swelling and choking him. And because there was no telling what ordeal he might still have to face, in the next hour, he formed his resolution and pulled his horse around. He rode back up the street until, at the first saloon, he pulled into the rack, and stepped down. The horse would stand. Keating simply dropped the reins across the weathered pole, not trusting his trembling hands to tie, and walked into the building on unsteady legs.

He was the only customer. When he ordered his drink, he thought the bartender looked at him strangely. He knew he must give something like the appearance of a very unwell man. He threw his money on the bar and managed to pour the rye and tossed it into his throat, and shuddered a little as its potency hit him. But it lent a strength that he needed. He took in a deep breath, and braced his shoulders within the boxed tweed coat.

The bartender, busy with his chores behind the polished counter, suddenly broke in on his musings with a question. "Say, Keating. Did you ever get ahold of Webb Toland, when you was in here earlier this morning, lookin' for him? Somebody said he took off for Copper Hill almost as soon as he got off the stage."

He scowled at his empty glass. "That's right," he said shortly. "That's what I found out."

"Way you talked, I thought maybe you was supposed to be havin' a meeting with him, or something."

"Oh, no. Just something I wanted to see him about. Toland's a busy man. I'll catch him another time."

He thought the bartender accepted this explanation, for the man nodded and turned away, busy with his wet rag on the polished hardwood surface. But to himself Keating thought bitterly, in remembered alarm: *You talk too much!*

This morning, coming into Antler expecting to meet Webb Toland and learn what success the promoter had had outside with his last-ditch attempt to raise needed funds, he'd known the answer when he learned that Toland had left town without even waiting to see him. He should have accepted the fact, not lost his head and gone looking futilely through the place, asking questions that had only served to draw attention to him. When the truth finally came out, and people learned how all Toland's grandiose schemes for the Copper Queen mine had collapsed, they might remember this morning. They'd remember Paul Keating's anxiety, and they might suddenly see a link that he'd been wanting desperately to keep concealed.

Damn the rotten luck!

A shaking hand spilled more whisky into his glass. Staring at it, he thought again of the golden pictures Toland had painted. He thought of the constant pressures Fern had brought upon him for those things she couldn't have on the bookkeeper's wage her stepfather paid him. With a weak man's predilection for blaming others, he cursed the pair of them. And then, unbidden, the image of Matt Winship rose before his mind.

Winship, as he'd looked with the rifle's sights notched on his unsuspecting body. And then the resistance of the trigger, the kick of the weapon, the sudden film of muzzle smoke that swept stingingly into his face. The memory set his hand to trembling again and he grabbed up the drink and threw it off, trying to drown the searing horror of it.

Panicked!—so Fern had called him, when he came galloping into the yard at Spur and babbled a confession of the terrible thing he had done. Panicked by the knowledge of what his unlucky association with Toland had done to him, what it would mean if old Matt were to learn his guilty secret. Panicked because, only the night before, the old man had said, "I ain't takin' no syndicate's offer for Spur, but just the same it'd be worth knowin' some figures to throw in their face if they come at me again. I'd like to go over them books with you tomorrow, son, and get me an idea just how we're standin' with the bank."

Winship was no fool. He'd know, if he looked at the figures, that they were all wrong. He'd have probed until he uncovered just what had happened to his money. And so, riding home to Spur, full of the thought of Toland's deceit and the depths to which it had hurled him, sight of Winship on the trail ahead had been enough to strike panic and terror into Keating, and put a desperate solution into his head.

He shuddered, the need of another drink rising strongly. But he had control enough not to succumb to it; he knew his limit. In despair he pushed bottle and glass aside and walked back out to his horse, trying hard to discipline his features and not to show to any casual passer-by a hint of the turmoil within him.

He turned into a side street where a small clapboard house stood well back among rustling poplars. A sign, fastened to

the pickets of the fence, said: MRS. LAURA PITKIN, DRESS-
MAKING. He saw at once that his wife had beaten him here,
and the sight of her mount waiting at the iron hitching
post beside the gate filled him with mingled emotions. He
didn't know if this was a good sign or a bad one. He pulled in
and dismounted, but then stood beside his horse with the
reins in his hands as he saw the door of the cottage open and
Fern and the Pitkin woman came out upon the porch, chatting.

They had been standing just inside the door, no doubt
watching for him. He lifted his hat to the dressmaker, and
got her birdlike, flashing-eyed nod in return. There was something about the woman that always repelled him: something
greedy and knowing in her black eyes, something secretive
in the tight mouth and the narrow, pointed face.

"Wednesday, then, for the fitting," Fern Keating was saying as she came down the steps to the path.

The pale head nodded, the old woman's glance darting to
the man waiting by the gate. "Yes ma'am. I'm real sorry I
have to make you wait again. I thought I'd have the dress
ready by today, but I couldn't get the thread I need."

"It's perfectly all right," Fern said, and flashed her such a
warm smile that for an instant Keating wondered. She was not
one to accept delays gracefully, or a needless trip to town.
Why then should she make the concession to a mere seam-
stress?

But his own needs and worries crowded the thought from
his mind. He waited impatiently as Fern came toward him.
When she walked through the gate and closed it behind her
he saw the smile quit her face to be replaced by another
expression. "You took your time getting here!" she whispered
coldly, as he moved to help her to the saddle. Then, with
him bending close to place his hands for her boot, she re-
coiled a little and he knew she had caught the whisky on
his breath. "I might have known!"

He shrugged the remark aside irritably. "What did you
find out?" he demanded.

She waited until he had lifted her up and she was settled

on the saddle, her full skirt smoothed across her thigh. Riding crop in hand, she looked down at his anxiously waiting face. "Matt isn't at the doctor's," she told him. "If his horse hasn't carried him in to the ranch by this time, I suppose he's lying out somewhere. Dead, perhaps."

Keating closed his eyes a moment. "If only we could know for sure!" He opened them again. His weak mouth twisted with the pain he felt. "He was good to me! To think that I had to repay him like this! I'll answer for it, and so will you!"

"Blaming me again?" she said sharply. "Because you got wild and lost your head?"

"Because it was you that got me mixed up with that grafter, that Toland!" he answered doggedly. "You made me dig into the books so deep there was no way to straighten them."

She swung her head, the coppery curls brushing the white column of her throat. "You wanted what Toland might have given us as much as I did!"

"Very well. We were both fools! But he isn't going to get away with this, either! He didn't have the nerve to meet me as he'd promised, and tell me the bad news. Well, I'm going right up there to Copper Hill and have it out with him!"

"Paul!" He was turning back to his own horse. He didn't see the look she gave him—the consternation, the sudden fear of what despair and whisky might lead him to. But then Fern subsided, biting her lip, and her fingers crept into the pocket of her skirt and touched the fold of paper they found there.

It was not the first such note Laurie Pitkin had slipped to her. The dressmaker had been serving a useful function as go-between, now, for many weeks. This note was unsigned, as of course they all had been. Still, she knew well every loop and downstroke of the strong, bold writing: "Tonight, at the usual place and the usual time. I must see you."

Yes, she thought suddenly. Let Paul take his useless ride up to the camp. It would be convenient, at that. Best to get him well out of the way, in this crazy mood of his in which al-

40

most anything could happen. "Suit yourself," she said. "But you can't leave me alone until we've learned something for certain about Matt."

He shrugged, not answering, as he pulled his horse around. There was a felt distance between these two, riding their horses down the slight hill from the dressmaker's house. They turned again into the wide, limb-littered main street. And there, all unexpectedly, saw the confused mill of horses in front of the hotel, and heard the excited shouting and a sudden muffled shot.

Keating pulled in so quickly that his nervous mount pivoted and Fern nearly lost the saddle, trying to avoid colliding with him. She heard his gusty exclamation: "What the devil?"

Someone on the sidewalk cupped hands to mouth and yelled the answer, in a voice cracked with excitement. "Hey! It's your paw, Miz Keating! Old Matt Winship! I heard somebody say he's been shot. They got him trapped in the hotel—Burl Hoffman, and Alcord, and their boys! Looks like they're set to smoke him out of there."

Jim Gary stood before the mirror in his room, smoothing back his long hair with the hard palms of his hands, eyes only half paying attention to the image in the watery glass. He was thinking of the expression on Tracy Bannister's face when he'd come back up the stairs after getting rid of Vince Alcord, and found her waiting, her cheeks drained, her eyes dark with apprehension.

"It's all right," he'd assured her. "Our friend decided to leave."

"You're certain?"

He nodded, and then as they stood there a sound had come from Matt Winship's room: a faint murmur of pain. It broke into the moment. It pulled the girl back to her concern for the injured man. She looked into Gary's face an instant longer, as though there were things she wanted to say. Then she turned and slipped back into the room and he stood and stared at the closed door before returning to his own drab quarters across the hallway.

Now he considered his unsmiling face in the glass and noticed how long it had been since a barber had touched scissors to that full and slightly grizzled thatch. He realized suddenly that he was seeing himself through Tracy Bannister's eyes and he shook his head, dissatisfied with this discovery, and walked over to the window.

It was midafternoon, he decided; three or four hours to wait, perhaps, until the stage left. An impatience filled him, for the time to pass quickly now and be over. He didn't like the things that had been happening to him. He feared he was becoming involved in something. He could sense the tendrils that were reaching to him from the affairs of this place, trying to weave and trap him in a web of circumstance. He couldn't afford to have that happen. He certainly would be a greater fool than he credited himself, if he let himself be swayed out of his purpose by the words or the smile of anyone he knew no more about than he did about Tracy Bannister.

Scowling over his thoughts, he stood looking down into the street and rolling a cigarette from the materials in his shirt pocket. He had placed the twist of paper and tobacco in a corner of his lips, and was reaching for a stick match on the washstand beside the lamp, when the knock came on his door.

His head jerked at the sound. For a moment he waited, his thumbnail against the match head, almost reluctant to answer. But when the sound didn't come again, he said finally, "Yes?" and the sulphur popped to life. He was putting the flame to his smoke as the door opened slowly.

It was the girl. She entered rather diffidently, with a fleeting and somehow apologetic smile. Hand on the knob of the opened door, she said, "He's resting," and indicated that other room across the corridor. "When he stirred I was afraid there might have been some internal bleeding."

"Not where he was shot," Jim Gary said gruffly as he shook

42

out the match and flipped it through the open window. "It's a good, clean hole. I told you that."

"I know," she admitted, and pushed a hand tiredly through her dark wealth of hair. "I—I'm afraid I'm still a little upset, with it all."

"Of course."

He regarded her through the film of smoke from the cigarette, which the draft of the open door sucked against his face. He knew there was something more on her mind, and he waited.

"I didn't get to thank you," she said, "for . . . what you did afterward."

"Your friend Alcord?" Gary shrugged. "He talked trouble but he didn't make much. He's mostly wind, I figure."

"Some of the others aren't."

"The others?"

"Burl Hoffman, for one," Tracy answered, with a hint of impatience in her voice, almost as though she had forgotten he was a stranger who knew nothing of the background of the trouble he had stumbled into here. "He's the leader, and I don't think he'll stop at bluster!"

"But who are these men?" Gary insisted. "What's their grievance against Winship?"

"It's simple enough. He's too big to suit them, and they're too little. That's what it comes down to. Myself," she added, "I've always thought that a man was small by nature, that you couldn't make yourself any taller by trying to cut down someone else to your own size."

He liked that; he liked the flash of scorn in her eyes as she said it. But he asked, studying her gravely while he dragged at the cigarette, "Would they hate him badly enough to risk murder?"

"You're thinking about the sheriff." The girl shook her head. "They're not afraid of George Ruby. And anyway, who else could it have been?"

He frowned. "It wasn't Alcord, I'm sure of that much. That was no act he put on for me. He saw the horse, and the blood

43

on the saddle, and he was trying to find out just what it meant. It tickled·him to think Winship might have been hurt, but he certainly had no previous idea it had happened."

Tracy didn't seem convinced. She said only, "Any one of the others could have done it."

"Did Winship say anything to indicate he might have seen who it was?"

"No. He was too far out of his head."

"But not far enough gone to stop him riding to you for help. You said he knew he'd be safer here than going to the doctor's."

"Or anywhere else. Yes, he'd always know that." The words died on her lips, suddenly. At something that came into Gary's thoughtful look, her own eyes widened. Color crept up from her throat, touched her cheeks. She tried twice before she managed to get out: "You're thinking of something that Vince Alcord said, about Matt Winship and me!"

Somehow, he couldn't meet her hurt stare. He looked at the burning end of his cigarette instead, put it back between his lips. "There's no need to explain anything to me!" he said gruffly.

"Meaning, you thought it was true!" He heard the break in her voice, and glancing up at her saw the shame in her eyes as she shook her head. "I suppose," she told him heavily, "there are lots of others who think so, then. I didn't know there'd been talk! But they'll have to think and talk as they like!" she added defiantly. "I owe too much to Matt Winship to turn against him. There's no one else who understands him, how alone he is. . . ."

He saw a shine of tears in her eyes. Embarrassed himself, he remembered something and said, to change the subject, "I saw a couple a little while ago, riding Spur horses. A young man and woman. Are they his kin?"

"That would have been the Keatings," she answered, her emotions settling. "She's Matt's stepdaughter. Her husband keeps the books out at the ranch, handles business details and paperwork. They're all the people Matt has since his wife died, three years ago."

Her look told him more than her words—told him that she had small use for that handsome and glittering pair. He considered this, as he turned and snapped the butt of his smoked-down cigarette through the window toward the street far below. He turned back, and his mind was settled and his manner changed. Firm and yet a shade apologetically, he said. "Miss Bannister, I've asked too many questions. I had no business taking up so much of your time with them, because they were none of my concern and in the nature of things they can't be."

He knew she read his meaning. She said quietly, "I understand. And I don't mind. You did help me. It gave you a certain right." But having said that much she paused, and Gary knew she was searching out the words for something else she wanted earnestly to say.

She took a step toward him.

"You're in trouble yourself," she blurted. "It isn't fair that there's no way someone could return the favor!"

"By helping me?" He shook his head, and a faint smile edged his lips. "Bad business! The men I mentioned—"

"The ones you're running from?"

Gary nodded. "They made that mistake. They saved my life. Now they're wishing they'd let me die! You've heard of the doings up in Mogul Valley?" he went on, prompted to talk about himself, against his better judgment, by something he saw in her face. "I was mixed up in that, as your sheriff guessed. You see, I'm just what Ruby thinks I am—a hired gunfighter. It's nothing to be proud of, nor was my part in in the Mogul Valley affair."

"You don't have to tell me anything," Tracy Bannister said.

"Somehow I want to. Maybe it's so you'll understand why I've got to be going on, this evening. The Planks," he continued, and a frown took shape between his eyes, "were on the other side of that fight. There was quite a gun battle, and

I took a bad one." He touched a finger to his chest, above the puckered scar.

"By all the rules I ought to have died of it. But when I woke up, I found that Boyd and Asa had taken me in. Six weeks they spent, waiting on me hand and foot, just because they couldn't watch a man die—not even one who'd been fighting for their enemies. They did a good job. Got me on my feet again."

Tracy was staring at him, frowning her puzzlement. "But I don't understand! Why would they be trying to kill you, now?"

"That's the rest of the story! You see, there was a third brother in that family. I'd made myself an enemy or two, on the other side, the one I was supposed to be fighting for. They wanted me, bad. And this other boy—Lane Plank, his name was—fixed up a deal to deliver me. For pay. But when he tried it—"

"You killed him?"

Gary nodded. "I didn't want to. He wasn't much of a man, not worthy to sit at the same table with a pair like Boyd and Asa. But he was their brother, and all they knew was I'd killed him after what they'd done for me! So now they want to find me. If we should meet over gunsights, they'll be playing for keeps."

"While you won't be able to," she finished. "Because you owe them your life. And that's why you're running! Isn't there anything to be done? Any way to make them understand?"

He shook his head and shrugged. "Don't worry about it. I've thrown them off my trail now, for a few hours anyway. I plan with any luck to lose them permanent."

"Then I wish you the luck you need!" she said earnestly.

"Thanks."

But her eyes were still studying him, still troubled. "And after you've lost them?" she persisted, with a directness that made him somehow uncomfortable. "You don't really enjoy this kind of life? A professional gunman—I just don't believe it! You're not the kind who'd take to it of your own choice."

"You're well acquainted with the type?" Gary suggested, his thin smile widening while his eyes chilled a little. He saw the look bring the color again into her face.

"I'm sorry. I didn't mean to pry!"

And then, before he could apologize or answer to the stiffness in her voice, the noise breaking in the street below drew him around quickly to the window.

There seemed almost a dozen in the mill of riders that had pulled up before the hotel. Some were already dismounting, while others held to their saddles in seeming indecision. Almost at once Jim Gary's raking glance singled out Vince Alcord's high-shouldered shape, and from this he knew what was happening even before Tracy's startled voice spoke, at his elbow.

"That's Burl Hoffman!" she exclaimed, and he knew she was pointing out the big sandy-haired figure who towered above the other horsemen, already giving orders. "And Priday Jones, and—Alcord's fetched the whole lot of them!" She swung away from the window, starting for the door. But Gary moved quickly and his hand closed upon her arm, stopping her.

"No," he said quietly, as her look raked his face. "Stay here. It begins to look to me that I'm not finished with this business after all."

Her quick protest followed him, unheeded, as he moved at a quick stride through the doorway and toward the stairs. He was already loosening his sixgun in the holster.

V

HE MOVED into the door and put his shoulder against the edge
of it, and for a moment none of the men in that mill beyond
the hitch racks seemed to notice him. It was Vince Alcord who
finally glanced his way. He stiffened, and with dark anger
flooding his face reached to drop a hand on Burl Hoffman's
shoulder, as the latter was about to swing from saddle. Jim
Gary saw Alcord's mouth form the words, "There he is now!
That's Gary!"

Hoffman slowly settled back into the leather. What Alcord
said must have carried, because the rest were turning to look
in Gary's direction now, and suddenly the noise and confusion
stilled. Gary stood and let his glance run over them all, sorting them out, deciding which were owners and which were
hands. And then their leader's voice rang a challenge.

"Don't stand in our way, mister! We're coming in!"

This Hoffman was a good-sized figure of a man, all right,
and he looked like a man governed by temper. He had a
ruddy face and scalp, that showed through thinning strands
of sandy hair that he combed in a saddle straight across his
head. His jaw thrust forward as though he expected someone
to take a poke at it. He had a restive intensity that he trans-
mitted to the big chestnut under him; it kept the horse moving edgily about. Like the man, the horse seemed ready to
explode.

Gary said calmly, "Come ahead if you really think you want
in bad enough."

Nobody moved. They were waiting on their leader, and as
he sensed this the redhead's scowl deepened. His eye touched
on the gun thrusting up from the stranger's hip holster, lifted
again to his face. His big shoulders stirred and he said, "All
right, Gary. I'll lay the cards out. You already know who we
are, I guess. Hoffman's my handle. This old-timer is Priday
Jones." He indicated a slight, small-boned man with a thick

48

shock of snow-white hair edging beneath the brim of his hat.

Gary only touched Priday Jones with a glance. "I don't need to hear names," he said coldly. "Just tell me what you want with the gent who's lying upstairs with a bullet in him." His mouth hardened. "Didn't take the bunch of you long to gather! What's the matter? Isn't one try at murder enough?"

Hoffman's angry jaw settled. "It was none of us who shot Matt Winship!"

"No?"

"No. But we ain't above using a situation somebody else has set up for us!"

"And who would you say *did* shoot him?"

"How would I know that? We ain't the only enemies he's got. Especially not since people have learned about the syndicate!"

"Syndicate?" This was a new one to Gary and he didn't hide his puzzlement. "*Now* what are you talking about?"

"Not that this is any of your business," Hoffman told him. "But it's some Eastern outfit. Back in Cleveland."

"Chicago, is what I heard," Vince Alcord corrected him.

The big man shrugged. "All right, Chicago. Word has it they're out to buy Winship's ranch off him. We understand he's ready to close a deal."

"You understand a lot, don't you?" Gary gibed dryly. "Do you know any of this for certain?"

"We intend to find out. And right now! We mean to have a plain answer from Winship as to whether he really intends throwing this range into the hands of some corporation."

"It's his ranch," Gary pointed out, "to do with what he pleases. But supposing the rumors are true?"

"We've told you all we figure to," Hoffman said. "Now you just get out of our way!"

Still the man in the doorway failed to move. He stood at ease, seemingly; but anyone looking closely at Jim Gary might have noticed the faint narrowing of his eyes, the slight stirring of the muscles along his cheeks. He said, "The odds

49

seem a little heavy. A crowd like this against one wounded man."

"It's your neck," Vince Alcord warned him, "if you try to buck this crowd!"

Then, from the head of the stairs behind Gary, Tracy Bannister's cry of warning rang sharply through the lobby: "Jim! Behind you!" It brought him pivoting against the point of his shoulder, as he whirled back into the room.

His gun lifted from holster in a single, unthought motion as he saw his danger.

A couple of men had entered by the hotel's rear door, while he was occupied with the rest out front. They had come silently into the lobby and only a few feet separated them from him. They were ordinary cowhands by their looks, but one already had a gun leveled and the other, at his heels, was even now pulling his revolver up from the leather.

Seeing Gary's sixshooter, they stopped like men frozen. The second man failed to complete his draw. Jim Gary let his gun settle on the other and told him sharply, "Drop that!" And when the man was slow about complying, he coldly and deliberately worked the trigger.

Sound exploded in the room. The man with the gun shouted in pain and fell back against his companion, grabbing at his upper arm while the Colt tumbled to the floor. "Move when I speak!" Gary snapped, real anger boiling in him. "Now, come here!"

This brought the pair to him, the hurt man stumbling and cursing the pain of his skewered arm, while blood began to redden the fingers that clamped it. His companion, white-faced and scared, was holding onto him and helping to guide his steps. Gary motioned them both out the door, drawing aside to make room for them to pass. "All right," he said then, turning back to the group at the hitch post, "whose men were these?"

The answer was slow in coming. They exchanged uneasy and frightened looks, and finally Burl Hoffman settled his shoulders and answered defiantly, "Mine."

"Then take them! And the next time anybody tries coming at me, front *or* back, he'd damn well better be ready to shoot first. Next time I won't be aiming for his gun arm!"

He had never been so furious, and there must have been something in his voice and in his eyes that carried fear to these men. Not one of them tried to meet his gaze. A couple hurried forward to help the man Gary had shot. Somebody said, in a shaky voice, "He's got to see the doctor quick! That arm is in a bad way!" For just an instant Gary felt a qualm of regret. He could have stopped the man, probably, without using a bullet. But his anger at the attempted trickery rose and utterly swamped this other feeling, and he shrugged it aside. He lifted his voice across the confusion in the street.

"Alcord!" he said, and the head on the mismated shoulders swiveled quickly. "What did you do with the bronc?"

"What bronc?"

"Winship's. The gray that I turned loose. I don't imagine you'd let it run, to show up at the ranch and get the Spur crew headed this way too soon!"

Alcord said gruffly, "I don't know nothin' about it!" But his eyes showed he was lying. And with the muzzle of his gun, Gary pointed to a hitch pole.

"He'd better be tied to that post inside of twenty minutes!"

There wasn't any answer. All at once the only interest seemed to be in getting away from there. The hurt man was being hustled off down the street, supported by his friends. There was a scramble for saddles, as the group broke apart and lost its unity. The whole town had come awake by this time, roused by the shot. A block distant, Gary glimpsed the fat sheriff heading that way at a puffing dogtrot, which was probably the closest George Ruby could get to a run.

Only Burl Hoffman seemed to have defiance still left in him. Face livid, he shouted Gary's name; he stood in the stirrups, the reins cramped tight in a grasp that made the restive horse under him fight the bit and toss its mane. "Whoever you are," Hoffman said as Gary turned his attention on the man, "wherever you came from, don't buy into this. We ain't always going to be so easy to stop!"

Gary measured him, unspeaking. Then, deliberately, he turned his back.

Tracy's heels tapped a light rhythm on the stairs as he came into the lobby. Her face was white; the hand she laid on his arm trembled with the strain of these last minutes. "Is it over?"

"For now, anyway," he assured her. "They lost their nerve. They talked when they should have been acting. It's a common mistake."

She closed her eyes and her breathing tremulously swelled her bosom. "For a minute I thought you'd be killed."

"I might have," he admitted, "if you hadn't warned me. Now they've sobered down, and with the town roused and the sheriff on his way I doubt if anything more will happen. So you can stop worrying. About him," he added, jerking his head toward the stairs that led above.

Tracy was looking at him again, and her blue eyes held concern. "But what of you, Mr. Gary?" she demanded. Only then did he realize that a moment ago, in the stress of excitement, she had called him by his first name. "You won't take any chances? You won't have more trouble with them?"

He shook his head. "I won't be here long enough. It's only a few hours till stage time." And, touched by her obvious concern, he gave her one of his rare smiles before he walked out of the hotel.

A few townspeople gave him curious stares. As he started along the street he heard his name shouted and knew that would be George Ruby. He walked on, ignoring them all.

He had spotted a faded barber pole fastened to the front of a small building down the street. He walked down there without hurry and found the barber standing in the open door. The man blinked and backed hastily as he saw the stranger turning in.

"I need a haircut," Jim Gary said.

"Yes sir, Mr. Gary!" The barber nearly stumbled over his

own feet, ushering him in. Gary stepped to hang his hat on one of the row of nails on the wall. He was working at the buckle of his gun harness when, through watery plate glass, he saw on the farther walk a couple of the men who had been with Hoffman in front of the hotel.

His hands stilled as he regarded them narrowly. Then, leaving the belt in place, he swung back to the chair where the barber waited, with comb and scissors and towel. He shoved his filled holster around to the forward part of his leg, and stepped into the chair. And when the big towel whisked into place covering his body, his hand rested on the butt of the holstered gun.

The muzzle pointed at the door.

When, a half-hour later, Jim Gary left the shop and walked back upstreet to the hotel, he saw that Matt Winship's gray horse now stood, saddled, at the tooth-marked and sagging hitch pole. A look of bleak satisfaction settled about his eyes and his mouth, seeing the effect of his threat: Vince Alcord, at least, had learned something from the events of the afternoon.

There were two other broncs at the pole, both fine animals, wearing the Spur brand. Gary studied them a moment before he recognized them, and then remembered he had seen the Keatings riding them into town earlier. The Keatings: the sullen, glittering young man, and the woman with her coppery hair and flawless skin and her direct, bold stare.

Gary shrugged, and walked into the lobby and up the stairs to his room.

There was no real hurry. He had no packing to do except to reassemble his roll. His saddle was probably where he'd left it, in the bushes behind the stageline corral. He still had time to kill, through what was left of the long summer afternoon, before the stage would be pulling out for Copper Hill.

The door of Matt Winship's room stood partly open and, hearing a rumble of voices within, he hesitated a moment. But now the door swung wider and a seedy little man came backing out, one hand on the knob and a worn doctor's bag in the other. "I'll look in again in an hour or so," Gary heard him say, "and find out how you're doing. Main thing you need is rest." Past his shoulder, Gary saw Paul Keating standing at the foot of the bed. Somehow that changed any thought he had about going in and he swung away instead toward his own room, hearing the doctor's footsteps retreating along the corridor.

But then Tracy Bannister was saying, "Will you come in a minute, Mr. Gary?" He turned to find her looking at him from that door opposite.

He frowned, reluctant. "Is it necessary?" However, he shrugged and she stepped aside for him, and now he saw Keating's copper-haired wife standing beside her stepfather's bed, a hand on the hurt man's shoulder.

Matt Winship had regained consciousness. He sat propped up with a couple of pillows against his back. His face, for all its weathered ruggedness, showed a pallor that was hardly darker than the neat, professional bandage with which the doctor had replaced Gary's own makeshift effort.

All their eyes rested on Gary as he walked in—Keating's, scowling and perturbed; his wife's, coolly curious. It was big Matt Winship who spoke, in a deep rumble of a voice that suited his massive frame.

"I understand I'm in your debt."

His eyes were blue, their contrast softening a little the rugged contours of the bearded face. They regarded Jim Gary with a level directness that he instantly liked.

Gary shook his head. "You're wrong. You don't owe me a thing."

"Tracy tells me," the hurt man persisted, "that you patched me up so I wouldn't bleed to death, and then kept the cur dogs off my hide, I'm grateful."

"There are things any man would do for another."

"Not just any man," Winship corrected him dryly. He nodded then toward the Keatings, who were watching all this in silence. "You've met my children? Fern and her husband Paul?"

Gary acknowledged the introduction with a brief nod that was not returned. He looked again to the man on the bed. "How you feeling?"

"Tired," said Winship. "Tired, like I never been in all my life! Funny what a little piece of lead can do to a man. Over fifty years I been a fighter." He shook his massive head. "Now suddenly it's like there ain't no fight left in me!"

Looking at Tracy, Gary saw the concern that grew deeper in her eyes as she heard what Winship said and the tone of his voice. Gary was watching her as the hurt man turned to his son-in-law. "Paul."

"Yes, Matt?"

"That syndicate," Winship said slowly. "I've changed my mind."

"What do you mean?"

"I'm takin' their offer!"

The reactions were varied and immediate. Gary saw Paul Keating's head jerk, with an undefined emotion. But it was Tracy Bannister who spoke, as though the words had been jarred out of her. "Oh, no!" she cried, and Gary noticed how the red-headed woman's glance lifted sharply to the other girl.

"It's a fair enough offer," Matt Winship said, his manner dogged and with a listless quality that seemed so odd in the type of man Gary had taken him to be. "Probably as good as anyone will ever make me for the ranch. And . . . I dunno. I been lyin' here thinkin' maybe I better play it safe and take this while I can.

"Ain't as though I had any real reason for holdin' out; ain't as though I wanted to pass Spur on to my family. It's been plain to me for a long time that they got no interest in takin' the place over when I'm gone—and why should they? Because it means something to me doesn't mean I should expect them to want to be saddled with it."

He nodded to himself, as though admitting the force of his

THE LURKING GUN

own arguments. The blue eyes, under their black brow thickets, turned on his son-in-law. "And so, Paul, I want you to have the books all in shape. And tell Ed Saxon he's to be ready for the syndicate inspectors so they can make range count of the stock."

Jim Gary happened to be looking at Keating as Winship said this, and so it was that he surprised a look on him that he could only interpret as startled shock. The young fellow covered up quickly enough, but Gary knew what he had seen and it left him frowning, wondering over a question he didn't quite put into words.

Paul Keating asked, after the slightest lapse of time, "When will this be, Matt?"

"Right away. Soon as we can get a wire off to Chicago."

"I see. Very well." Saying it, Keating glanced at his wife. Whatever he was looking for from her, he didn't get it. A tiny muscle worked for an instant at the corner of his mouth; a small, pulsing pit of shadow against the smoothness of his too-handsome face. Then abruptly he turned on his heel and went out of the room, without even a glance for the other people in it.

Fern watched him go. Afterwards, a coppery highlight played across her hair as she placed her long-lashed stare on Jim Gary, considering him in a way that made him think she might be wondering if he had noticed anything in her husband's manner. Gary met her look but it lasted for an instant only, before she again faced the man in the bed.

She said, "I think you're absolutely right, dad. You've worked hard enough and long enough. It's time you thought about something else for a change. Time you enjoyed what you've worked for!" She gave her stepfather a smile and laid a hand on his knee. "Now don't give the ranch a thought. You just lie there and get well. Paul will take care of everything. I'll see that he keeps his mind on his duties."

She was gone, then, her footsteps light as she followed her husband from the room. Looking after her, Gary heard Tracy's indignant exclamation: "Enjoy what you've worked for!

How can *she* know! How can she pretend to think she knows what Spur has been to you?"

The hurt man smiled a little. "You don't want to be unfair. Fern never took much to this life out here. But then, her mother didn't either."

"You just can't sell the ranch!" Tracy cried. "You can't *do* it!"

"What else is there?" Matt Winship demanded, with a shrug. "With the hounds snappin' at my heels—"

"You can fight! You've always been a fighter. It isn't like you to lie down!"

He shook his grizzled head against the pillow. "I dunno. I feel like they've killed something in me. Maybe the next time they'll finish the job. I don't think I could stand a next time!" The heavy-lidded eyes closed. "I'm an old man, suddenly. And I want to be let alone!"

"Oh, Matt! Matt!" Suddenly Tracy was beside him, going down on her knees by the bed. She flung an arm across his chest, pressed her head against him. "It breaks my heart to see you like this!"

Jim Gary watched the man raise his arm about her, the big hand closing upon her shoulder in an affectionate embrace. It was no more than a fatherly one, surely. But Gary frowned a little as he looked away, remembering what Vince Alcord had had to say about this man and this girl. And why, he wondered suddenly, should it make any difference to him, one way or the other? What if she actually was the old man's mistress? It could be no concern of his.

"Your name's Gary?"

Matt Winship's words, directed at him, brought his eyes back to the man. Gary nodded briefly. "That's right."

"I like your looks," Winship said bluntly. "Tracy says you're quite a scrapper. I was one, myself—reckon I know the signs." He paused, a question printed in his eyes. "Wish I was free to ask you another favor."

"Such as what?"

He asked only because he was curious, expecting almost

any answer. He was totally unprepared for the one he got.

"I need someone at Spur, to take charge while I'm laid up. Get things ready for those syndicate buyers. Keating can handle the paperwork. And there's Ed Saxon, who's a good enough range boss. He'll be able to get the stock shaped up for a range inspection. But I need somebody with more to him than either of those."

"You aren't offering *me* a job?" exclaimed Gary, the words jarred out of him. "You never even laid eyes on me before?"

"I size a man pretty quick," Matt Winship said with quiet confidence. "Saxon would like to be foreman but he's a lightweight, and that ain't good enough! You've seen the men who hate me; you seen what they already tried. Maybe you know by now that they'll do anything at all to keep this sale from going through. The man I need is one who can hold 'em off until it does. From what I've seen, he could be you, Gary! Say the word and I'll write a note that will give you authority to ride out there right now and take over."

Tracy had pulled back and was staring at him, still within the circle of his arm. "No, Matt!" she said hastily, a little too loudly. "He can't!"

"I'd pay well. I'm pretty desperate."

"You don't understand!" she insisted. "You're asking something it's impossible for him to give!"

A frown etched itself into Winship's craggy brow. He twisted his head to look at the girl, and then back again to Gary. He said gruffly, "Reckon there must be something here I don't know about. If I spoke out of turn, Gary, just forget I said anything!"

Sunlight lay full upon the hurt man and on the girl who knelt beside him with his arm about her shoulders. Jim Gary looked at the two of them, wondering suddenly what he was doing in this room, in this town.

And he was astonished to hear his own voice saying quietly, "That's all right. If you think I'm the man for the job, Winship, I'm ready to take it!"

VI

HE HAD finished packing and was just pulling tight the lashings of the saddle roll when Tracy Bannister knocked and entered. She placed her shoulders against the door and stared at Gary a moment, watching the neat, deft movements of his hands. "Why did you do it?" she asked finally.

Jim Gary shrugged. "I figured he needed help pretty bad, to ask a total stranger. Being needed is kind of a new experience for me! Besides, I like the man.

"But it seems like a hell of a service," he added with a frown. "I can't think he really wants to sell. Still, those are my orders."

"And those other men? The Planks? You're in danger every minute you stay here, without taking on Matt Winship's enemies!"

"I've always pushed my luck pretty hard. Maybe it will stand a little more pushing."

He picked up the blanket roll, slung it across his shoulder, and took his hat from the bed. "Do me a favor?" And when she nodded: "Since I haven't got a horse of my own, I'm going to take Winship's gray for the ride out to Spur. My saddle's stashed away in the bushes down near the stageline corral. Could you have somebody dig it out and fetch it up here to the hotel, to keep for me?"

"Of course."

"Which is the road?"

"You take the north trail from town. Bear right when it forks at the crossing of Antler Creek. It's a ten mile ride from there."

He nodded his thanks. "I'll find it." But in the doorway he halted, as she stood aside for him. "Oh, one other thing. Did Winship give you any idea where this ambushing took place?"

"Why, yes. He said it was just as you pass the turnoff of the Ute Flats Road. You'll see a signpost. He told me the shot seemed to come off the ridge." She frowned, puzzled. "Why did you want to know that?"

"Just to be asking." He left her with that, and went down the lobby stairs and outside.

The two Spur-branded horses the Keatings had ridden were now missing from the hitchpole. Winship's gray gelding stood alone, hipshot and idly pawing the drying mud. Gary slung his roll behind the cantle and strapped it down. He was testing the cinch when he heard his name spoken and, turning, recognized the small, white-haired man who came striding toward him.

It was one of the Alcord and Hoffman crowd, the rancher he'd heard called Priday Jones. There was something ill-at-ease in his manner as he came to a halt, his hands shoved into hip pockets of his denims, and scowled up at Gary through white thickets of bushy brows.

Gary met his look coldly. "You want something with me?"

"Look, Gary!" the old man blurted. "I'm sorry about what happened awhile ago. I'm not a quarrelsome man. But I got to look after my own interests, and I figure my interests are the same as the others'. I have to go along."

"What were you planning for Matt Winship if you'd got your hands on him—to finish what that bushwhacker tried?"

The old man colored but shook his head emphatically. "Oh, hell no! Nothing like that! Actually, we were thinking we could take him out of the hotel and hold him awhile, until we got satisfaction."

"Kidnap him, you mean?"

"Well, something like that. A crazy idea, I suppose, when you think it over. But we're desperate enough to try anything."

"Wouldn't your sheriff have had something to say about it?"

Priday Jones's waxen cheeks bunched in a look of distaste. "George Ruby," he said, "ain't too much of a man."

"I don't suppose it even occurred to you that, in his condition, you might have been committing murder by trying to move someone as badly shot as Matt Winship!" From the way

60

the old man slid his eyes away, uncomfortably, Gary knew he'd hit solidly. He added, "Just what did you think you were going to get out of him?"

"Well . . ." The old fellow hesitated, and then plunged ahead. "You heard of Ute Flats?"

Gary shook his head. "Nothing more than the name."

"It's a good stretch of graze, well-watered. The way it sets it makes sort of a buffer between Spur and the rest of us. It's a bone of contention between us and Matt Winship. Not only do we all need the grass, but we're thinkin' ahead, to that syndicate moving in. You know how it is with them big outfits! We'll trust 'em a lot better, if we can only get control of Ute Flats before they take over Spur.

"The Flats is open range," he went on. "Never did belong to Winship, except as a matter of prior usage. And if Winship won't hand it over peaceably, we'll use other means."

"Then you'll have a fight on your hands!"

"Maybe not. With Matt laid up, it leaves Ed Saxon and that weak sister of a son-in-law to hold down Spur. We'll never have a better chance." He hesitated, and his faded eyes set a speculative regard on the tall stranger. "But meanwhile, I got me an idea."

"Yeah?"

"It's pretty much dog eat dog around here just now, and my teeth is kind of blunted with age. I admire the way you handled yourself, facing the bunch of us there a while ago, and the way you used that gun you wear, when the situation demanded. George Ruby or somebody was telling me you wore that gun during the trouble up in Mogul Valley. If you ain't got other commitments and if your price ain't too steep, I'd like to see you wearin' it for me!"

Jim Gary looked at him coolly, through a long and silent moment. "You're offering to hire my gun?"

"Plain as I can put it. Never paid gun wages before, in a long and pretty busy lifetime; always fought my own wars. But a man don't always know if he can even trust his own friends! What's in your holster could make a lot of difference, come a real showdown."

Gary looked behind the words, read the real note of anxiety in them. Another time, he might have been a little sorry for this old fellow who was trying to run with wolves like Burl Hoffman and Vince Alcord. But his loyalties were already engaged, and Priday Jones was aligned on the wrong side with those who would take advantage of a man laid flat on his back by an ambush bullet.

He shook his head. "Sorry," he said bluntly. "You spoke a little late. I've already been hired."

The news took the old man hard. It straightened him like a blow, and the hands jerked out of his hip pockets to dangle aimlessly at his side. "Who by?" he demanded hoarsely. "Not—"

"Exactly!" Jim Gary had whipped the gelding's reins free of the gnawed pole and now he stepped into the saddle, favoring the pull of muscle in his half-healed chest. From the gelding's back he looked down at the other man, gave it to him straight. "I've signed with Winship. I'm rodding Spur."

The old man's mouth dropped open. His seamed face sagged and looked suddenly very sick. And Jim Gary left him like that, touching his bronc with the steel and swinging away from the rack.

He rode up the street, falling into a canter and splashing through the sky-reflecting pools of rainwater. He knew that within the hour all Matt Winship's enemies would have heard the news. That suited him. Let them take whatever warning they would from it.

The rain had done wonders for this land. It had brought out a flush of green on the bare, autumnal sweeps of thin-soiled range; in the hollows, water had collected and thirsty cattle gathered there to stand hock-deep. Nearly every dry arroyo had its miniature torrent of chocolate-brown runoff.

It would be gone in a few hours, of course, most of it sinking into the thirsty soil or finding its way to the few drainage streams. Still, the range was better for it, however brief.

Gary followed a plain trail, and when he reached Antler Creek, half-drowned willows along its turbulent course told how much it had risen above its regular level. The gray was edgy about taking the crossing but he encouraged him with a word, and they made it without trouble. Beyond, remembering Tracy's instructions, he swung his bridles toward the better-marked right-hand fork. This wasn't really necessary, because the horse knew it was heading home and it took the trail of its own accord.

There was considerable travel over this trail, and the sign failed to tell him much. He kept riding steadily and only pulled up when he came to a second forking, which was the one he had been alerted for.

As Tracy had promised, there was a faded signpost, indicating that the secondary trail he saw snaking off through the juniper led to Ute Flats. He sat saddle a moment, staring slit-eyed through brilliant sunlight in the direction of the Flats which, according to Priday Jones, was a prime bone of contention between Spur and its neighbors. Afterward he turned his attention to the low ridge that flanked the main trail here. He studied it, in silence broken only by the wind that sang in the junipers, and the whistle of a meadowlark somewhere.

The ridge was nearly bare: pink, shaley rock studded with low clumps of brush. No end of places, there, for an ambusher to lie and draw his bead on an unsuspecting victim.

Gary shook his head. He could waste hours on that bare-ribbed hill and find no clue. Nor would it matter very much, which one of Matt Winship's enemies happened to have been the one that tried to kill him. The real, vital damage was done.

He rode on.

At the end of the ten miles Tracy had estimated, the wagon road topped up out of a shallow barranca and there, suddenly, lay the ranch, its buildings tucked into the shelter where two bare ridges formed an angle. The main house was a big one, built of logs and fieldstone, and seemingly over a period of time, as though Winship had kept adding to it as he prospered from small beginnings. There were barns, and sheds, and a large bunkhouse with a kitchen. There was also a good-sized system of corrals. Everything looked business-like and trim, and as he rode in Jim Gary saw every evidence that Spur belonged to a man who thought a lot of his property.

In brief, it had everywhere the plain stamp of big Matt Winship. It had been built of his sweat and his years of loving effort, and the idea that it should be sold now to an impersonal corporation didn't sit too easily with Jim Gary.

Except for a dribble of smoke from the kitchen stovepipe and the cook's voice raised in some mournful cowboy dirge as he clattered around in there, Gary at first saw no sign of anyone. But then the clear note of a hammer striking on anvil began to sound, and he followed this around to a small three-sided frame shed that was the ranch smithy.

Here, fire glowed redly in a portable forge and three men stood about a saddled horse that was getting a hasty shoeing. They looked up as Gary rode toward them and at once all activity ceased. The puncher who was doubling as blacksmith, with a leather apron tied on over his jeans, let the hammer rest as he stared at the rider, and particularly at the gelding with the Spur brand on its flank.

It was a young fellow with a wild thatch of yellow hair who spoke. "Why, that's the old man's horse he's riding! Where'd you get him?" A rifle was booted on the saddle of the animal that was being shod. Quickly the puncher slid it out and swung the muzzle toward Gary, as the latter reined in. "Mister, you better start talking!"

The third man knocked the rifle barrel aside, shaking his head at the young fellow's rash anger. "Take it easy, Cliff." This was an old-timer, nearly as old as Priday Jones himself. He was a little stooped with the years, his head as round and dark as a nut. But the eyes that looked at Gary were sharp and shrewd. "He must have some kind of a story that makes sense, or he wouldn't dare ride in like this. Let's hear what it is."

"Thanks," Gary said dryly, and dismounted. The youngster, Cliff, held his rifle slanted toward the ground but his eyes were smoldering. Gary directed his words to the oldtimer, who seemed to have a monopoly here on cool common sense. "The name is Jim Gary. I'm here because Matt Winship sent me."

"On his own horse?" The old fellow's eyes narrowed. "What's happened?"

"Somebody tried to kill him."

There was a shocked reaction—first, disbelief, and then a rush of stammered questions. Gary proceeded to give them the facts as briefly as he could. When he was done all three stared at him in silence. Finally, the old puncher said, "We still don't know what *you've* got to do with this."

"There's something here that will explain. That is, if you know Winship's handwriting."

He handed over the note Winship had scrawled for him, and watched while they gathered close to read it. As one man they finished and raised incredulous stares. "It's his hand, right enough," the grizzled puncher said heavily. "Otherwise I'd never believe this! Selling out to the syndicate—and hiring a stranger to do the job!"

"I'm not sure I do believe any of it!" the towhead muttered.

"Easy enough to check. Go in and ask him. You'll find him in bed, at the hotel."

The oldster shook his head as he handed back the piece of paper. "It's the truth, I reckon. Though it ain't easy to accept. Pete Dunn's my name, Gary. These here are Cliff Frazer and Hack Bales."

"Glad to know you." Gary offered his hand and shook with old Pete Dunn and with Bales, the blacksmith. But Cliff Frazer only looked at the hand, his cheeks drawn tight with suspicion, the rifle still clutched tightly. Gary's mouth hardened but he didn't make an issue of it; he couldn't blame the kid for the way he felt. He withdrew the hand and said, "Will one of you take care of the horse?"

"I will," Hack Bales said, picking up the hammer again. "Soon as I finish here."

"All right. Now, where's the nearest telegraph office?"

Pete Dunn answered. "Reckon that'd be Elko."

"Winship wants a wire of acceptance got off to the syndicate. I'd better be getting it written, and tomorrow morning somebody can ride with it." He looked around at the silent ranch buildings. "What does Winship use for an office?"

"Yonder." Pete Dunn indicated a tacked-on wing of the main house. "Everything's there—all the books and records, anything the syndicate'll need to know." His mouth was a grim white line, his voice heavy with bitterness. Gary thanked him with a nod.

He started to turn, then held up. "As soon as Ed Saxon gets here, I'm going to want to see him."

"That's one thing you can count on!" Cliff Frazer said and showed his teeth in a mirthless grin. "It's gonna take more than a piece of paper to convince Ed that some stranger's moving in over him!"

Gary looked at the youngster sharply, and then saw Pete Dunn's confirming nod. He shrugged. "That's how it'll have to be, then."

From what Matt Winship had said about the current top rider, he had been led to suspect he might have to face some argument from this Ed Saxon when he learned the new state of affairs. But the look these men gave him made it appear more as though what he'd have on his hands would be a fight. . . .

The study was a big room, big enough to have its own stone fireplace, with the stuffed head of a lobo wolf mounted over it. Matt Winship's throne was a swivel chair that stood in front of a scarred, broad-topped desk holding a blotter and pens and pencils and a rack that contained a half-dozen much-smoked pipes. As he sat in the chair, a man

66

could make a quarter turn and look out through a window onto the ranch yard, and the wide dun sweep of rangeland stretching out toward the hills clouding the horizon.

Jim Gary sat for a long time staring at that view, thinking of the hours big Matt must have spent here, judging how much it undoubtedly meant to him, how much he must hate to give it up. The more he learned about this man, the more Gary disliked the job he had undertaken to do for him.

On a smaller desk, that stood beyond the fieldstone fireplace, Gary found a stack of account books and briefly thumbed through them. They were kept in a spidery hand and were replete with ink blots and careless erasures. Paul Keating's work, he judged. The figures meant nothing to Gary, for he had no knowledge of accounting. Keating would have to fill him in on the details of Spur's finances.

He shoved the ledgers aside and returned to the big desk, took pencil and paper and laboriously worded the telegram that would have to be sent to Chicago in the morning.

It was late as he finished and stood the paper up against the pipestand, and now the first sounds of arriving horsemen brought his attention to the window. He sat and watched the Spur crew ride in on the tail of the day's work, through the golden glow of sunset.

There were a dozen of them. They came off the range singly and by twos and threes, converging on the home ranch over as many different trails. They formed a clot around the corrals as they took care of their horses and ran them into the trap. Then the men came tramping toward the buildings, and there was something in their collective manner and in the looks they turned upon the main house that told Gary the news had spread: they'd all heard of the stranger who had arrived with word of Matt Winship's ambushing, and of his own authorization to take charge.

Here was one phase of the job he wasn't particularly looking forward to, but it had to be got through, one time or another, and better to have it done than to leave the men stewing in rumors and growing resentments. He stubbed out the cigarette he had been smoking. Leaving his hat on the desk, he stood and left the house.

Emerging, he saw a man approaching along a graveled path that led from the bunkhouse area. As Gary appeared, the man halted. Beyond, the Spur riders hovered about the doorway of their quarters, gone motionless and attentive. There was almost no sound as Gary closed the office door carefully behind him, and then paced forward through the deepening gold of the fading day.

The man in the path stood and let him come.

He was a stocky, tightly-knit shape—a man in his thirties, blunt-featured and with a stubborn, honest look about his brown eyes and wide mouth. Just now he was scowling, in a dogged and forthright show of dislike. His eyes met Gary's challengingly; he made no move to step out of the way.

Coming to a halt in front of him, Gary said, with a nod toward the men before the bunkhouse, "This the whole crew?"

The other only looked at him for a moment, without answering. Then he turned his head deliberately, glanced at the silent group and back again. "I reckon. All that'll be coming in tonight."

"Good. I'm Jim Gary. While we're together, I've got some things to tell them."

He started forward, to step around the other man. But the latter set his boots and brought up a hand, the blunt fingers against Gary's chest and blocking him. "You'll do your talking to me!" he said. "I speak for the crew. Saxon's my name. I'm top rider with this outfit.

"So I understood," Gary answered levelly, not letting any trace of anger into his voice or his answering look. "Matt Winship said I'd find you the most valuable man on the payroll. And I suppose, actually, it's for you this note is intended."

As he spoke he was taking the scrawled paper from his shirt pocket and offering it to Ed Saxon. The puncher barely flicked it with a glance. Next moment he batted it out of Gary's fingers, so that it skimmed and fluttered to the path.

And he said, in a tone that carried sharply in the sunset quiet, "I don't give a damn what the boss may have wrote on that paper! He must have been out of his head. He's got all the crew he needs, and I reckon I can rod it as well as some nobody he never laid eyes on before!"

An angry tightening bunched the small muscles of Gary's jaw, but he ironed it out again. He dropped his hand to his side, and said calmly, "Winship told me you'd feel this way. I can understand you might resent being passed over, but that's how he called the play. After all, I'm only taking orders, myself. Sorry if you don't figure you can cooperate."

Saying which, he turned away from Ed Saxon and moved to walk around him and on to the bunkhouse. But with a quick sideward step the puncher again confronted him, and this time Saxon's furious stare was inches from his own. "Maybe you don't hear so good, mister! I said you give no orders to this crew!"

I'll give my first one right now," Jim Gary said quietly. "Stand out of my way!"

Ed Saxon's fist swung directly at his jaw.

The blow was telegraphed in the leaping, angry shine of the man's brown eyes and the quick lift of his chest. Gary's forearm lifted and fended it aside, and the puncher was left wide open for the answering blow that took him on the side of the head. Ed Saxon was knocked spinning off the path, and hit the dirt in a loose sprawl.

He was surprised but this failed to stop him for more than an instant. He loosed a bellow of rage and at once the drive of his boots sent him springing up and charging straight for the man who had flattened him.

Gary squared away to meet the attack. They were well matched. Gary was an inch or so the taller, but Saxon was solidly built and bound with hard, firm sinew and muscle while Jim Gary himself was honed down by his recent bout with illness. So he knew he had trouble on his hands, and that his best hope lay in staying out of the puncher's reach and making his own efforts count as quickly as possible. He moved faster than Saxon. But the man's reaching hook missed him and threw Saxon off balance with the force of his lunge, and Gary threw a fist at him and felt the ache as his knuckles struck the bone of the man's forehead. Saxon fell back, blinking his eyes.

But he was only surprised, not actually hurt. He swore, dashed a hand across his eyes, and lunged at Gary with both clubbed fists swinging. Giving ground before him, Gary felt one of his bootheels turn on gravel. He stumbled, steadied himself, and in that helpless moment a blow like the drive of a piston sledged him full in the chest.

Agony went through him, a burning that told him the half-healed bullet wound had been wrenched open. He gasped and took a second wallop across the side of his face, that rocked his head on his shoulders.

They stood toe to toe, then, slugging. At the first exchange of blows the men from the bunkhouse had come running. They crowded around the fighters, and Gary had no doubt all of them were cheering Ed Saxon on. He heard shouts of: "Cut him down to size, Ed!" "Show the bastard up!" Grimly, Jim Gary stood and paried blow for blow, trying to break again through the other's guard and find a vulnerable spot.

But now the pain in his upper body was swelling with every savage blow. He could feel the steam leak out of his muscles. He lost his hat. Sweat plastered his hair against his forehead. His arms felt leaden and his knuckles seemed to bounce off the other man's toughly muscled shape.

A second piston-stroke found that spot of torture high on his right chest. This time it seemed to drive right through him. And this time, the watchers must all have seen he was hurt. Someone—it sounded like the young towhead, Cliff Frazer—shouted triumphantly, "You got to him that time, Ed! Finish him!"

The red tide of pain, receding, left a numbing blackness. Desperately Jim Gary willed strength into his arms; they were too heavy. His head rocked. Blows rained on him. And then he was falling, and the hard earth came up and struck him with solid force.

As from a great distance, voices spoke:

"He made out to be real tough, but Ed licked him easy!"

"Sure caved, all right. Reckon this will change the Old Man's notions of him, when he hears."

Gary tried to speak, tried to stir. He could do neither. Then another voice—the old-timer, Pete Dunn—breaking in on a sudden tone of alarm. "Ain't that blood, there on his shirt?"

"Hey! Pete's right, the guy's bleeding!"

Hands worked at his shirt buttons, ripping it open. Somebody swore. "Why, that's a bullet wound!"

"And only about half closed," Pete Dunn said. "The fighting tore it open. No wonder you licked him, Ed! Standing up to you with a thing like that in him—Well, he's a game one, that's all I can say!"

Ed Saxon cried, in a tone of horror, "But how was I to know? He never said—"

"You never asked!" Pete Dunn retorted sharply. "Well, are you gonna just leave him lay there? To bleed to death?"

Hands were under him then, lifting him. And as they raised Jim Gary off the ground, the last gray of twilight seemed to fade. Consciousness ebbed and then darkness swept cleanly over him.

VII

AT LEAST a dozen times, in her lonely waiting, Fern Keating heard a sound which brought her hurriedly to the door of the shack, certain at last the man she looked for was coming. Each time ended in disappointment that drew her nerves tighter with frustration and suspense. Then, as sunset painted the range and the sky, iron shoes struck an echo from a stretch of shale rock and she sprang up from the chair by the table, where she sat with empty hands. She was in the doorway as Webb Toland rode into view.

Now that the waiting was over, she stood with a hand at her throat and impatience roweled her cruelly. It seemed to take forever for the red roan horse to thread its way up the slope, through the thin stand of pine whose trunks were dyed to a rich red by the glow of the setting sun.

"I've been waiting for hours!" she exclaimed, and there was frantic urgency in her voice and in the hands that clutched at him as he dismounted. "I thought you'd never come."

The darkly handsome face drew into a frown. "But I said in my note it would be tonight."

"I know, I know. I couldn't help it. I was so anxious to see you—to learn what happened."

"Happened? What do you mean?"

"Why, in Denver, of course!" She almost shook him. "Did you get the money?"

He shook his head. The failure of his mission was already ancient history as far as Toland was concerned, so that he had almost forgotten she didn't know. His own busy mind was already ranging far ahead; he never looked back. "No," he admitted curtly. "I couldn't raise it."

"Oh, Webb!" She backed away, staring at him, aghast. "Then what about the mine?"

"It wouldn't have mattered anyway. I've had some expert opinion now, on the amount of flooding in the lower drifts.

72

My first estimates were wrong. It would be too costly an operation trying to reclaim it."

"But the money I talked Paul into giving you?"

"I can't return it just now. I'm sorry."

Her eyes brimmed with tears of anguish. "Later will be too late!" she insisted. "Can't I make you understand? Paul's out of his head with worry! He—" She corrected herself just in time. "Somebody shot the old man this morning, on the road to town. Now he's made up his mind to sell to the syndicate. It means the books will have to be examined. The whole story will come out."

"Are you worried about Paul?" he cut in, his eyes hardening. "If you are, then I suppose I've been wasting my time!"

"Don't say that!" She seized his arm convulsively. "You know I love you. Only you! Paul means nothing any more. But think of the scandal! He's so weak! When it's found out the money's gone, he'll blurt everything. He'll say that I told him to take it and put it into developing the mine. Before the thing's finished, the whole range will know about us!"

"There'll be no scandal," Toland assured her sternly. He had no intention of confessing that only a matter of an hour or so ago he himself had been ready to panic. Right now the saddlebags on the roan held the few possessions he'd cleaned out of his safe and desk in the office at Copper Hill, everything he owned. With the mining venture proven to be a fiasco, he had returned from Denver able to think only of meeting Fern here at the shack, talking her into running away with him, tonight, and leaving the rubble of his scheming behind.

But in the past half-hour, something had happened to change the whole course of his thinking.

"I ran across Burl Hoffman on the way up here," he said. "Hoffman told me all about Winship being ambushed. He told me more. He said the old man had hired himself a foreman, some gunslinger that suddenly showed up today."

The woman's eyes widened. "Not Jim Gary? I didn't know! It must have been after I left town."

Toland regarded her with sharpened interest. "You've met this fellow? What did you think of him?"

"He's a wild man! He fought with Vince Alcord and threw him into the street. And he shot one of Hoffman's riders. . . ."

Webb Toland nodded to himself, and his mouth took on a tilted smile of satisfaction. "Good! Good! He certainly seems to have stirred up the animals! Alcord and Hoffman and the rest of them are ready to fight, before they'll see a syndicate take over Spur. And with a roughneck like this Gary throwing his weight around, they'll be in a mood to fight even harder. Can't you see the opportunity for us in that?"

Fern stared in complete bewilderment. "For us? I'm afraid I don't follow you."

"With a stronger man than your stepfather at the head," he explained patiently, "Spur could be twice as big as it is. Even now it's worth many times over what he'd likely get from that Chicago outfit. Certainly you don't want him selling, not when there's a chance of building Spur bigger than it's ever been!"

"What chance?" She shook her head. "I still don't understand!"

"It's very simple." He took her by the shoulders. His voice was eager and intense, but he spoke slowly, almost as though he were explaining a problem in addition to a child.

"Hoffman and the others can't really buck an outfit the size of Spur, especially not with some tough gunman running it. They'll be broken, and leave Spur to pick up the pieces. Matt Winship will end up with an empire on his hands, whether he particularly wants one or not."

"But how does that help *us*? What about the books? How can Paul explain the money that should be there and isn't?"

"He won't have to. The sale will fall through. Eastern money isn't going to knowingly buy into a range war. As for Jim Gary, he probably doesn't know a debit from a credit; and besides he's going to have his hands too full to worry about figures written in a ledger. So you see, it give us the time to find some way to cover up the shortage.

"I said there'd be no scandal. I meant it! I'll let nothing hurt you, sweetheart."

She was in his arms again and their lips met, long and lingering, as he stilled her questions with his kiss. They were questions he wasn't ready yet to find answers for, though in in his own mind he already saw many possibilities.

Today Matt Winship had nearly died. In an all-out war with his neighbors, who would question too seriously if another ambush bullet proved more successful? Fern would be left as his only heir to the enlarged Spur that Toland saw rising out of the embers of the coming range dispute.

And, should there be any doubt of its outcome, Toland had a good half-dozen gunfighters in Copper Hill who could be used effectively wherever needed. With Fern Keating in love with him, he didn't see how he could fail to come out on top in the confused shape of events ahead. He'd come out with something far more valuable than some played-out copper mine.

There was Paul Keating—no problem! He could be gotten rid of at any time. And . . . oh, yes. This foreman at Spur, this gunman—Gary, was that the name? He was a cipher, at the moment. He might need more careful handling. But Webb Toland had no intention of letting some fiddle-footed gunslinger stand in his way when the time showed itself ripe for taking over Winship's ranch, and Winship's daughter.

For minutes after he woke, Jim Gary tried to imagine where he was and then, as memory of the fight with Ed Saxon came to him, decided he must be in the bunkroom at Spur. Morning light lay on the empty room, with its wood-framed bunks built in double tiers against the walls, and the gear and clothing hanging from nails. There was a deal table and chairs, a space heater sitting in a box of cinders. Beyond a partition, male voices and a clatter of dishes sounded in the kitchen that occupied one end of the building. The crew was at breakfast.

He tried to sit up and made it on the second attempt. His face and body felt like one huge bruise, testifying to the beating he'd taken. The ache of the bullet wound in his chest was a piercing throb. He examined it, found someone had bandaged it tightly. The cloth was unspotted, so he didn't seem to be bleeding any longer.

Whoever put him on the bunk had removed his shirt and his boots, but not his trousers. Gary looked around, saw his boots nearby and hooked and dragged them over. He worked them on and then got carefully to his feet. He was in good enough shape, he thought, considering.

As he stood holding to the timber of the bunk, the connecting door opened letting in a burst of noise from the kitchen. He turned, and saw Ed Saxon standing in the doorway looking at him.

For a moment neither moved or spoke. Then Saxon closed the door, shutting away the racket. His face was sober and he was ill at ease. He said, "How do you feel?"

"I've felt worse."

"It took nerve walking into a fight when you knew you had that bullet hole in you!"

Gary shrugged. "I couldn't see myself using it as an excuse to duck out."

"I still wish I'd known," Saxon said heavily. "I don't like beating hell out of a man and then finding he was already hurt."

"Forget it! The important thing is, I may have got licked but I'm not backing down. I'm still foreman here and I still intend to give the orders. So where does that leave us?"

He saw a flush creep upward through the man's blunt features. Ed Saxon was the one to break gaze. He said, doggedly, "It's no pleasure half-killing a gent as nervy as you, Gary. But, by God—"

He never finished. A shout from the yard outside broke in on him: "Ed! Where's Ed Saxon?" A hard-ridden horse plowed to a stand. In the adjoining kitchen, there was a hurried trampling of boots.

Ed Saxon gave Jim Gary a startled look. "Sounds like Johnson, the rider we had with the herd on Ute Flats."

Gary was directly behind him as he rushed out. The rest of the crew were gathered around the newcomer and his lathered horse. He was wild-eyed, bareheaded. His holster was empty and one shirtsleeve was blood-soaked.

"It's Alcord and Hoffman, and that crowd!" Hack Bales relayed the word as Saxon and Gary hurried up. "They've hit the Flats. Driven off our herd and tooken possession!"

"When was this?" Ed Saxon looked white beneath his tan.

"Gray light," Johnson answered. "They planned it good. Priday Jones and a couple of his men jumped me while I was still in my blankets; they held me and the rest started movin' our stock into the junipers. Claim they're gonna hold onto the Flats come hell or high water or a syndicate army!"

Jim Gary frowned. "Wouldn't the law have something to say about this? What's the sheriff's office for?"

"That fat-headed George Ruby?" young Cliff Frazer snorted. The veteran puncher, Pete Dunn, nodded sober concurrence.

"Spur don't actually own the Flats," the old man pointed out. "It's a matter of customary usage. By every right except legal title, the Flats belong to Matt Winship for as long as he continues to run cattle on them. But Sheriff Ruby isn't going to stick his neck out as long as he can find a technical excuse!"

Ed Saxon was looking at the blood on Johnson's shirt. "Who shot you?"

"It's no more'n a nick. One of 'em tried to stop me when I seen my chance and made a break."

"What are they doing now?" somebody wanted to know.

"Time I left, they was digging in and putting up breastworks. You ask me, they're getting ready for a battle!"

"Well?" Hack Bales demanded. "And what about it? They gonna get one?"

All eyes turned toward Saxon, then. He felt the weight of their looks. He seemed suddenly tormented by doubt: he ran a hand across his cheeks, down over his mouth, and the hand was trembling. And looking at him, Jim Gary understood the man.

Saxon was a good cattleman—an honest plodder, excellent for seeing that the routine of a working ranch was accomplished. But here, faced with an emergency, he was floored. And this was precisely what Matt Winship had foreseen, when he decided to look elsewhere for a foreman.

Gary settled his shoulders. Without preliminary he took over the reins. With the first word he spoke, leadership passed to him like an invisible mantle.

"Whatever they think they're going to do," he said, "we have to catch them while they're off guard, before they expect it. Everybody get horses and guns. But remember," he added sharply, "those guns stay in the holsters until you get orders!" And to Hack Bales he said, "Rope out a bronc for me, will you, Hack?"

"Yes, sir!" Hack said eagerly. "You bet!" And he joined the general rush for the corral. Gary turned to the man named Johnson.

"Have the cook take a look at that arm," he ordered. "See if it needs a doctor. Otherwise, you're to stay here at the ranch."

Johnson didn't argue. But as he started away, he paused to give the stranger a closer look. "Never seen you before," he said. "You must be this Jim Gary, that I heard Priday Jones mention. The new foreman Winship signed on?"

Gary only nodded. As Johnson walked off toward the kitchen, Ed Saxon asked him, "What's your plan?"

There was no trace of hostility in the question or in Saxon's blunt, honest face. As abruptly as that, he seemed to have accepted Gary's right to authority, his position of leadership. Perhaps the truth had been borne home to him that, in the showdown, he himself was no leader.

"No plan," Gary had to admit. "We'll just see what the

THE LURKING GUN

thing looks like when we get there. You have to be ready to improvise, and then move fast, to carry out whatever you've thought up!" He added, "I better finish dressing."

"You sure you can ride? You in shape for it?"

Gary answered the anxious question with a nod. In the bunkhouse he found his roll and dug a clean shirt out of it. He didn't bother with shaving. Remembering he'd had no breakfast, he went next door to the kitchen and let the gimp-legged puncher who served as the ranch cook pour him a china mug full of coffee. He drank it standing in the doorway, munching at a bacon sandwich as he watched the activity in the yard. The crew members worked fast and efficiently to catch up their mounts and cinch saddles into place. Rifles slid into saddle scabbards. Sixguns were checked for loads and replaced in holsters.

Suddenly, in an upstairs window of the main house, Gary saw a woman looking silently down on the scene.

It was Fern Keating. A dressing gown was belted at her waist and, as she leaned with hands on the sill, her long, copper-colored hair lay unbound upon her shoulders. The morning sun shone on it as on a new-minted penny. She was a beautiful sight, Gary admitted, the coffee cup forgotten for a moment in his hands.

Then he saw Hack Bales hurrying up, leading a skewbald gelding. Prompted to his immediate duties, Gary put the woman from his thoughts. He finished off his coffee, handed the cup to the waiting cook, and hurried out.

"Mount up!" he shouted, and rose into the saddle as leather creaked and horses stomped restlessly in the yard. "Let's ride!"

The Spur crew left the ranch yard in a rush and a quick thunder of hoofs. They rode into the morning. The last thing Gary saw, glancing back, was the coppery glint of the woman's streaming hair, framed by the window.

They were a sober group and they rode quietly, without much talking, thinking of the thing that lay ahead. Once, as they halted to breathe their mounts, Gary found himself next to Pete Dunn and something prompted him to ask the old puncher, "You known Matt Winship long?"

"Longest of any man here," he answered promptly. "Rode with him in Texas and the Indian Nations. And I was at his stirrup the day he come into this Nevada country and sized it up as likely cattle range."

"Then you must have been with him all through the building of this ranch."

"Every step of the way! And I can tell you, it's been the nearest thing to his heart, 'specially since his marriage went sour for him. He's sunk a lifetime and a fortune trying to improve the land and the stock. Wait till you see the special herd of Black Angus he's got spotted over by Buck Ridge! That cost him real money." The old man shook his head, his face clouding. "And now to give it all up. . ."

"Sounds to me you think pretty highly of him."

Dunn stabbed him with a clear, undimmed gaze. "No finer man ever forked leather! You take what he done for the Bannisters—"

"Tracy Bannister, you mean? The girl at the hotel?"

"Her and her pa, Luke Bannister. He was another old hand of Matt's. He got throwed and rolled on in the Spur corral, by a bad cayuse Matt had ordered him not to ride. Now, any other boss would of said it wasn't none of his blame, and washed his hands of it. Not Matt! He paid all the hospital bills, and when we seen that Luke wasn't gonna be able to get out of a wheel chair, let alone ride, Matt still took care of him.

"Made a down-payment on that hotel in Antler, footed all the bills till Luke and the girl could make a go of it. And since Luke Bannister died he's been with Tracy like she was his own daughter!" At a thought, the old puncher's mouth pulled down. "Wish to hell she *was*, in place of that step-daughter his wife left him! Josie Winship was a real good woman, but that red-headed first husband of hers must really have been a pip! Handsome as hell, most like, and no damn good at all!"

They rode on, after that, and Gary mulled over what the old man had told him.

He knew a strange sense of relief. Pete Dunn's opinion of Fern Keating didn't concern him. But what he'd had to say about Tracy Bannister eased his mind more than he would have cared to admit. He told himself he had never really believed the nasty hints Vince Alcord had passed about the girl. Even so, it was good now to hear the facts concerning her relationship with Matt Winship—the real link between them, the true basis of her gratitude.

Ute Flats was actually a grassy depression in the sparse juniper forest, hemmed by low hills to the west, and on north and south by slanting rims. It would be a couple of miles from end to end of it, and perhaps half as wide. In a land of fairly dry range, its acres of graze that were well watered by a natural collection tank could be valuable indeed.

"Johnson said they were digging in," Ed Saxon remarked. "I guess I see what he meant."

He stood with Gary on a rise that gave them a view toward the Flats, where water glinted under a high, cloud-dotted morning sky. Silently Jim Gary studied the near end of the depression, and the wagon trail that snaked toward it through the sage and juniper. Where this trail dipped onto the Flats, the low rims drew together, like a funnel, making a gap of little more than a quarter of a mile. And there he could see tiny figures frenziedly at work.

They were throwing up breastworks of dirt and stone and timbers hauled down from the rims. They had a pair already built, flanking the road, and were starting on a couple more which would tie in with the protecting rims and make a barricade that could be held against an attack from the direction of Spur.

"Looks to me like Burl Hoffman's thinking," Saxon said dryly. "He was a corporal in the Army Engineers, once. This is probably his idea of a real military maneuver!"

"Could be a pretty good one," Gary answered. "That is, if we gave them time to finish. But I don't think we're going to!"

The puncher looked at him sharply. "You already got a notion?"

He nodded. "Could be. This juniper gives pretty good cover, and the ground's still too soaked to raise a dust. How long would it take you and half the crew to circle wide and come in on that south rim, without letting yourselves be spotted?"

Saxon computed, eyeing the lay of the land that was cut by arroyos and overgrown with the twisted, bushy trees. "Fifteen minutes, maybe."

"I'll give you twenty. This has to be timed or it won't work. Who's your most reliable man with a rifle?"

"Cliff has a good eye, and he's cool."

"The kid? Will he follow orders?"

"Sure."

"Then let's go." And he led the way back down the rise to where the rest of the crew were bunched, waiting for the word.

The shaggy, blue-berried junipers were washed to a brilliant green by the recent storm. As Jim Gary picked a careful way through them, with Pete Dunn at his stirrup and five members of the Spur crew trailing, the red hide of an occasional steer showed among the twisted trunks—part of the herd Matt Winship's enemies had thrown off its customary graze on the Flats. The porous earth soaked up hoof-sound; Gary rode with a confidence that they would be giving the enemy no warning of their approach.

The trees grew almost to the dropoff of the rim. He dismounted, turned his reins over to one of the men, and moved forward on foot for a look, dropping to all fours as he neared the edge.

The wide depression of the Flats lay directly below him, here. Long waves of shadow flowed across it as clouds intermittently shuttled over the face of the sun. The only stock in sight was a small bunch of saddle horses belonging to the men who were sweating and toiling in evident haste to get the logs and stones piled up and tamped with dirt to complete the barricade.

Two of the men—the only ones with guns in their hands— stood guard at the breastworks that were already completed; they were keeping an anxious watch on the approach through the junipers, waiting for the attack they knew they had invited by their move in ousting Spur cattle from the Flats.

Only one thing was wrong with their calculations: The enemy was already at their backs.

Directly opposite him, now, on that other low rim some four hundred yards to the south, Gary saw movement as Ed Saxon and his half of the riders came into position. Cautiously he lifted an arm, wig-wagged and received an answering signal. Afterward he drew back, got to his feet, and returned to the riders he'd left waiting. Rising to the saddle, he shouted, "Let's go!"

They came down onto the Flats with a rush, dust and gravel spurting under braced hoofs. As they finished the drop Ed Saxon and the rest of the crew were breaking over the opposite rim. Both groups hit the level, then, and were spurring directly toward the work party at the barricade. They fanned out as they rode.

The surprise was complete. Their busy picks and shovels making a covering racket, the workers failed even to hear the horses until they were nearly on top of them. Whirling, they stared helplessly at an enemy sweeping in on their rear, and were too surprised at first even to drop their tools.

Gary's attention was on the two guards. His sixgun was in his hand and he flung a shot that dropped one of them with a smashed leg. The other, suddenly realizing he was on the wrong side of this barricade they'd put up with so much effort, turned and made a desperate effort to fling himself to cover across the top of it.

But now Cliff Frazer carried out the precaution Gary had taken against this. Out in the junipers, a rifle cracked. A steel-jacketed slug raised a film of dirt from the top of the breastworks and whined skyward. The guard, losing his nerve, dropped his carbine and slid back down the mound of wood and stone. By the time he scrambled to his feet, the Spur riders were menacing the entire group. Shovels and crowbars were flung aside and hands were quickly raised.

Altogether, two shots had been fired. The only one to be hurt was the man whose leg Gary's own bullet had skewered.

Young Cliff Frazer came whooping in along the wagontrail, out of the junipers, spurring his pony and brandishing his smoking rifle. Pete Dunn was crowing as the Spur crew disarmed their prisoners. To a scowling, black-haired man named Marshall who, as Burl Hoffman's foreman, seemed to be the leader of the detail, he said, "What's the use building a fort, if you let your enemy sneak in and grab you from behind?"

Marshall, glowering beneath his brows, said nothing. But another man retorted, "You just didn't give us time to finish. Half an hour more and we'd been ready for you."

Ed Saxon gave Gary an openly admiring look. "You're dealing with a gent who ain't going to give you any extra half-hours!"

But Gary, for his part, took no share in this. He wasn't wholly satisfied. Looking at Marshall, he saw the way the foreman's scowling glance seemed to keep returning to a spot on the far western edge of the Flats, where the ridge of rocky hills edged it. Never a man to take any victory for granted, he suddenly took warning and said sharply, "Ed! You and Cliff watch these birds. Have one of them do something to keep this one from bleeding dry." The rest he signaled to follow him.

A notch in the ridge yonder commanded his attention. He knew that was where the trouble would come from and he spurred directly toward it. While the Spur riders were still some fifty yards short, the first rumble of plodding hoofs and clacking of horns and mutter of bawling cattle began to sound Then a steer broke into view, up among the rocks and brush, then two more hard on its tail. Legs braced against the downward pitch, the lead steer saw the horsemen suddenly blocking the way ahead and he hauled up, swinging his horns. He tried to turn back as the other steers crowded down on him.

Jim Gary's sixgun snapped flatly and the lead animal buckled at the knees and rolled over on his side, and Gary saw Burl Hoffman's Box H brand on the steer's flank. The cattle immediately behind bawled in fear and stopped short. Farther up in the notch, a man's voice shouted faintly in alarm.

More cattle appeared, pressing hard on those in the fore. No orders needed to be given. The Spur riders opened fire, and several more steers dropped. By then, a racket of bellowed fear rose above the echoes of the guns. In the narrow gap, cattle were turning, trampling, goring in their frantic anxiety to escape from what waited for them at the foot of the pass.

Suddenly horsemen were visible, shadowy figures trying to buck the snarl of frightened beef. One of them was Burl Hoffman. He saw the defenders at the foot of the slant and at once a gun in his hand was blazing. Jim Gary fired back, saw the hat jump from the man's sandy hair. Other guns opened up on both sides.

For a matter of minutes there was real madness in the rocky throat of the gap. Steers bellowed and tried to climb over one another. Men shouted, fighting to hold their horses steady. Burnt powder spread its stench.

Actually the fight was quickly over. One of the attackers took a bullet and, dropping his gun, clutched for the saddlehorn. His horse, turned by the pressure of steers trying to escape in the direction from which they'd come, swung broadside against one of the other riders. In an instant, the confusion was too great for any attack to continue.

Burl Hoffman, the last to admit defeat, took a last angry shot at Gary and missed, then savagely he swung his horse's head and he too was gone, in the wake of his men. Echoes died among rocks and brush. Now all that remained behind were a half-dozen dead steers, stiffening where the bullets had dumped them—a plug of slaughtered beef that should block further attempts by Spur's enemies to drive their cattle onto the Flats, through this route at least.

The fighting had been so brief there had been no time for the Spur crewmen to dismount. Empty gun smoking in one hand, Jim Gary settled the frightened skewbald and said, "That's that! Now we'll move our own stock back where it belongs and turn loose the prisoners, without their guns. And we'll keep a three-man guard here, until we're sure they aren't going to try anything like this a second time."

"Gary!" somebody cried in a tone of horror. He looked, and only now realized they hadn't got through this encounter unscathed.

For the old-timer, Pete Dunn, lay in the dirt where he had fallen from his saddle. When Jim Gary got to him, he found the man still alive but unconscious. Blood pumped from a bullet wound in his chest at an alarming rate.

At this price, victory had come high indeed.

VIII

WITH shadows thickening among the town's buildings—though the last light of day made the sky overhead the color of steel—the figure of the man swinging out of saddle before the saloon had a familiarity about it that hauled Jim Gary up sharply. He said, aloud, "Boyd Plank!" Next moment, as he got a better look, he saw there was really nothing more than a similarity of shape. But the experience had been a disturbing one.

As he rode on to the hotel hitchrack and there dismounted to tie, he was thinking that events had so far taken over his mind as to make him lose all sight of his own personal affairs, until reminded by an accidental look at a casual stranger.

Alarmed by this, he stood a moment with his hands upon the tooth-gnawed smoothness of the tie-pole, thinking now about the Planks and wondering what might have happened to them—wondering if they wouldn't have guessed by now that they'd missed the trail somewhere. Then he shrugged; he was committed here, and he couldn't do justice to two worries at one time.

He'd known what he was doing, and risking, when he took on the chore for Matt Winship. So be it.

Lamps were burning in the lobby. The night clerk was already at his post behind the desk. Gary, looking for Tracy Bannister, shook his head at the man and went to look into the dining room, where a handful of townspeople were scattered among the tables. Not seeing the person he wanted, he was about to turn away when a voice spoke his name sharply and halted him, drawing his eye to a table where two men were seated.

It was the fat sheriff, George Ruby, who had spoken. He was pushing back his chair, which creaked under his gross weight. He made a move to rise but then stayed as he was, for Jim Gary had altered his course and was crossing the room

87

toward him. Gary touched the second man at the table with a brief glance, still so preoccupied with his own thoughts that he didn't immediately recognize the dark features. But when he saw the tawny eyes he remembered Webb Toland, from that single meeting at the stage station. Their eyes met briefly, and then Gary returned his gaze to the sheriff's scowling face.

"Well?" he prompted.

"What's this I heard about some gunplay out at the Flats this morning?"

"I wouldn't know what you heard," Gary replied shortly. "There's probably no telling, since I suppose you heard it from the other side!"

The sheriff didn't like his tone. His flabby cheeks colored and he said quickly, "Far as that matters, I've known Burl Hoffman and Vince Alcord for a long time, and I've known *you* about two days. I warned you I didn't much cotton to some strange gunslinger riding in here from nowhere, and turning a bad situation into open warfare!"

This view of the matter was so blatantly unfair that Jim Gary shrugged, seeing no point in arguing it, or bothering to point out that Spur's enemies had made the initial move by their attempt to grab Ute Flats. "All right," he said curtly. "So you warned me." He turned to leave.

"How's Pete Dunn?" the sheriff asked gruffly. His tone held real concern, and Gary paused long enough to give him an answer.

"Doctor was with him a couple of hours. Did everything he could. But the old fellow's still unconscious."

Ruby wagged his head. "Bad. Damned bad! Can you tell me who it was put the bullet in him?"

"No," Gary admitted truthfully. "There was a lot of lead being flung around. How'd the other side make out?"

"Nothing to fuss about. A skewered leg and a rib smashed. Doc had better luck there."

"I'm not apt to waste tears over them." Concerned as he was about Pete Dunn, he had little mercy for those who had followed Burl Hoffman in his unprovoked attack on what, by custom and usage, was recognized to be legitimate Spur graze.

Webb Toland's eyes regarded him across the rim of a coffee cup. "You sound pretty cold-blooded, my friend," he observed, and got a hard stare from Jim Gary.

"And what's *your* stake in this business?" Gary demanded bluntly.

The other lifted a shoulder. "None at all," he said, "being a mining man myself." He set the cup down, appearing to take no particular offense at Gary's manner. Laying money beside his plate, he rose and took an expensive flat-topped hat from the seat of an empty chair.

"Well, my stake," Gary said in the same cold tone, "is the promise I made to a man lying, hurt, upstairs in this hotel. When I sign on a job, I try to do it. And if I think the man I hire with is in the right, then any man who works against him has to count me for an enemy!"

"And I take it," Webb Toland murmured, with what Gary read as an edge of mockery, "that you figure yourself as a fairly bad enemy?"

"As bad as I can manage!" He added, with a curt nod at George Ruby, "Good evening, Sheriff." Not waiting to discover if the lawman had anything more to say, he turned on his heel and walked back through the lobby archway. He left the dining room in complete silence, with everyone's eyes following his straight, solid back.

In the lobby he confronted Tracy Bannister. She must have heard the exchange, for her face was stern, her eyes troubled. "Were you trying to pick a fight in there?"

He shook his head tiredly. "I dunno. I dunno what I was trying to do. Your sheriff rubs me the wrong direction. And there's something about that other gent that doesn't set with me, either."

"Webb Toland?" She made a small gesture. "I can't really say I blame you. But he's on the sideline, as far as Spur's troubles are concerned. He at least is one man you shouldn't need to worry about. So why let him upset you?"

"A good question, I suppose." He didn't know what nagging thing it was that worked at him—something he had seen in the pale eyes that made him feel this Webb Toland wasn't really as disinterested as he pretended.

The girl was watching him with an anxious look. She said, "Come in the office."

It was the room that lay behind the lobby desk, a small room taken up by a rolltop desk and a couple of chairs. In the doorway, Jim Gary glanced back into the lobby and saw Webb Toland walking into the night, pulling on his hat. Gary frowned thoughtfully as he closed the door.

From this room, Tracy managed the running of the hotel. It was neat, like everything else about her, but it had been furnished by a man. Probably Luke Bannister had consciously copied Winship's study at Spur, aping the tastes of the man he had admired, and Tracy had left things untouched when her father died.

She took the swivel chair behind the desk and watched Jim Gary slack into the deep leather chair opposite and drop his hat upon his knees. "You're really tired, aren't you?" she said.

"It's been a long day." He didn't bother to add that ever since the fight with Ed Saxon the half-healed wound in his chest had been aggravating and troublesome.

"Tell me what really happened at the Flats. I've had nothing but rumors."

His account was brief, succinct. He ended, with a glance toward the ceiling, "Has *he* heard anything of this?"

"Matt?" she shook her head. "Not from me, and I haven't let anyone near him except Dr. Walsh. The doctor said he shouldn't be told anything to alarm him, or put him in a worse mood."

"How is he?"

"Physically good enough. I think he could go back to the ranch if he wanted to bad enough. But he doesn't seem to

want much of anything. That bullet did more to hurt his
spirit than his body. It frightens me to see a man like him
suddenly beaten."

Gary rubbed a palm across his jaw, feeling the shaggy
stiffness of unshaven beard. "Damn!" he exclaimed, an explosion of breath. He went on: "I know what you mean!
I've seen that special herd of Black Angus that means so
much to him. And the crew.

"Not a man of them that doesn't want to fight this thing,
instead of sell. Especially after the business at the Flats. This
evening they're out on guard, working overtime voluntarily
to make sure there aren't any more such surprises." He hesitated. "The real reason I came in," he said then, "was that I
thought—if he really knew what's been going on—"

"He might change his mind?" she finished. "Get mad enough
to fight?"

"Something like that."

She shook her head, a crease of worry forming between
her brows. "You can try it if you like, I suppose. But I hope
you won't take the risk."

"Why's it a risk?"

"The strange mood he's in—I just don't know. He'd have
to be told what happened to poor Pete Dunn. And I'm afraid
that that, on top of everything else . . ."

She let it go unfinished. Jim Gary looked at her for a long
moment in silence. Then he dropped his eyes to his boots.
"Well," he said finally, "you know him better than I do."

"I'm sure I'm right!" Something made her lean in her chair
and place a hand on his wrist. It was hard with muscle and
bone, weather-roughened. "I'm sorry," she told him earnestly.
"But I *do* know Matt Winship. He's a stubborn man. He
hired you to do a certain thing. He's going to expect you to
do exactly that, and nothing else."

"To take part in dismembering a fine ranch," he interpreted,
and he swung irritably to his feet and prowled to the window, slapping his hat aginst his knee. He stood a moment
with his boots spread and his head shot forward a little, peer-

ing sightlessly through the glass into the growing dark outside. Tracy watched him, and when he suddenly swung toward her again she saw the hardness that had come into his jaw, and into the set of his mouth.

"I better tell you this," Jim Gary said curtly. "I wrote the telegram he ordered me to, telling them in Chicago that they had a deal." He spoke as though the words tasted bad to him. "I wrote it, but then I tore it up!"

She stared. "You had no right!"

"Maybe. But I'm a stubborn man, myself! I can't send that kind of a wire, whether Winship likes it or not! He'll have to send it himself. I'll hold the line against his enemies, until he's on his feet. If he still wants to sell then, that's his busines."

Tracy said, "Don't you see you're taking a terrible risk? You'll be facing his enemies, and you'll be going against direct orders!"

"I have to take the chance," he retorted. "If Winship doesn't like it when he finds out, that's too damned bad. But still better than if he'd think it over and be sorry—too late!—for a decision he made when he was flat on his back with a bullet in him!"

Her breast rose on a long, slow breath. She shook her head, the hair glinting softly in the lamplight. But she said, "Very well, Jim. I'll say nothing more. I give you credit for doing what you think you must. And I'll be praying that you're right!"

"Thanks," he said gruffly. "For now, I guess I'll be riding. I have to check the guard at the Flats, before heading back. And there doesn't seem much point in discussing anything with Matt tonight."

A moment afterward, he left. And for a much longer time, Tracy Bannister remained seated at her desk, staring with brooding, sightless eyes at the place where she had watched him standing, before the darkened window.

Paul Keating, in the lamplit study at Spur, with the hopelessly botched account books spread before him, was lost in a bad state of funk. Knowing there wasn't any whisky in the house, he wished for a drink with an intensity that made his hands tremble. His nervous system had taken too many shocks in these last few days, too many ups and downs that fluctuated too violently between tremulous hope and total, engulfing despair.

The worst moment had come yesterday when, alarmed by Matt Winship's announcement of his plan to sell the ranch, he'd raced the miles to Copper Hill to locate Webb Toland and pin him down to some definite statement about the money. But at the mining camp he'd found Toland come and gone, his office empty, the desk and safe hurriedly ransacked. People he'd questioned had told him alarming news. It was rumored now that Toland had been advised the Copper Queen was a hopeless proposition, that all his reports had shown the tunnels were flooded past any hope of reclaiming.

Certain of the worst—that he'd been swindled, left to face the wrath of his father-in-law—he'd returned to Spur this morning nursing desperate thoughts of suicide. And had learned from his wife about this man Jim Gary, being appointed foreman, with the job of pushing through the sale of Spur to the syndicate. Fern had tried, with ill-concealed scorn, to shame him out of the despair the news threw him into.

"Will you listen to reason, Paul? What is this Gary, but an illiterate gunslinger? If you can't pull the wool over his eyes, you're even more a fool than I think you are!"

"But I'll never fool a syndicate lawyer! One look at those books—"

"It may never happen," Fern had cut in mysteriously. "Worry about the syndicate lawyers when you see them walking into the office."

Whatever might have been in her mind, he could get nothing more out of her. She'd been less than reassuring. As for Gary, he hadn't even seen the man yet.

Ranch headquarters was silent at this late hour. Practically the whole crew, or so he understood, was out riding range against further attempts like the one at Ute Flats. The

93

windows were closed and a small blaze crackled in the fireplace. A chill that came with the setting of the sun had warned that summer was ending and fall was nearly on them. When a mutter of running horses began to swell out of the night, it was some moments before Keating's distracted mind registered the sound.

His head jerked up suddenly. The sound was unmistakable. Even as he got to his feet a swarm of riders swept into the yard. He heard the thunder of the hoofs; the hoarse bawling of voices. When the first guns began to roar, he understood. This was an attack!

A first knotting of terror gave way to fear for his wife. He found himself running from the study, across a hallway and into the main portion of the big house, calling her name. Empty stillness echoed him. The outer noise swelled to a crescendo, muffled by these thick walls that seemed to tremble with the pound of hoofs on hard-packed earth, the slam of gun echoes.

A window went out, close beside him. He dropped to all fours and crouched, shaking, as broken glass sprayed him and a shard of it ripped his cheek. No sound at all from the room upstairs, where Fern had retired an hour ago claiming a headache. Pushing to his feet, Keating shouted her name from a tight throat and then groped through darkness to the stairway, went stumbling up them two at a time.

Her door was locked. He pounded on it and rattled the knob, calling. Thought of her lying wounded, perhaps even dead from a flying bullet, sent his shoulder ramming hard against the wood. It was a sturdy slab but with the third lunge the lock pulled loose and the panel sprang inward. Keating grasped the edge of the doorjamb to steady himself, as he stared toward the bed.

Enough moonlight came through the window to show him it was empty. Wherever Fern was, she wasn't in this room.

His mind limped and stumbled, trying to understand and, in his confusion, failing. Then a flurry of gunshots in the yard carried him to the window. He stared below, incredulous.

It was madness! Mounted men spurred at will through the yard, raising dust and banging guns. Over at the bunkshack a couple of Spur hands were firing back, from cover—the crippled cook for one, he supposed. Perhaps even Pete Dunn had dragged himself off his bunk to put up a fight, so far as he could. But it wasn't enough.

Above all the other racket, he thought he recognized the voice of Burl Hoffman shouting hoarsely, "Burn 'em out! Burn 'em out!"

Already, one of the sheds was in flames, spreading a wind-whipped, ghastly light over the scene. Smoke and dust rose cherry-red. Torches made circles of fire as the attackers brandished them. Even as Keating watched, one let fly and a firebrand lobbed end-for-end, in a crazy pattern. Next moment came the smash of a downstairs window as it hit.

That sound broke him from his dazed inaction. "Oh, my God!" cried Paul Keating, in a throat that felt scraped and dry. He whirled and ran wildly from the room.

A hellish glow already showed at the bottom of the steps as he stumbled down them. Fire had seized on heavy drapes at the broken window, was licking toward the ceiling. The torch, rolling, had spread oily flames clear across the room. Heat and smoke caught at him.

There was nothing he could do here. He edged past the fire, and then shaking legs carried him again through the hall and back into the study, to stare wildly around. On pegs above the mantelpiece was Matt Winship's rifle. Paul Keating hurried and snatched it down, and with untrained motions checked its load.

But he was no gunman. He had no business in a fight! Helpless, he stood in the middle of that hated room, that held so many evidences of the father-in-law whom he so strongly feared. He listened to the hullabaloo in the night outside, and even with a gun loaded and ready, he knew he could take no part in the defense of the ranch.

And then his eye lit on the open ledger, on the other

account books that held the proof of his downfall. He coughed on acrid smoke that swirled through the hallway door. He looked at the small box safe in the room's corner, and suddenly it was perfectly clear to him what he was going to do.

It was no worse than what Webb Toland had done, he thought, picturing the empty safe in the office of the Copper Queen. Even bluff, confident Webb Toland—who Fern had often told him, scornfully, was twice the man Paul Keating could ever hope to be—had cut his losses and run when the hole he dug for himself proved too deep!

Keating could act when his course was set, and there was a certain cunning in him that his wife might have found astonishing. First he pulled open all the drawers of Matt Winship's big desk, as a hurriedly rummaging intruder might do. The box safe presented no problem. He'd often thought a petty thief could pry it open at will, using the fireplace poker.

He spun the dial hastily, and squatting before the box he scooped greenbacks and a sack of coins into the pockets of his coat. He got the poker then and took a moment to batter the door and the lock, completing the illusion of a forced entry. The sounds he made were lost in the continuing racket outside.

Smoke swirled thickly now, stinging his throat to rawness. He was held for an anguished moment in a paroxysm of coughing, as he clung to a corner of his own scarred desk. Afterward, driven by a desperate need for haste, he proceeded with the rest of his program.

He heaved the desk over. Account books and ledgers spun to the floor in a fluttering of leaves. Taking the burning kerosene lamp, he stood looking around to make certain of his arrangements. Then he lifted the lamp and slammed it down, hard, into the mess of fallen books and papers.

Burning oil spattered and pooled. Blue flame licked at the ink-blotted pages that had cost him so many hours of anxiety and toil. But not fast enough. He needed a cross draft. Quickly he hurried to a window and ran it open. Chill night air spilled into the room, bringing the racket of the yard outside. And now the fire leaped, beginning to eat greedily at whatever it could reach.

Hastily, Paul Keating grabbed the rifle and rushed through the hallway door, Sparks floated redly about him; past the living room archway he looked into the heart of a roaring furnace. He gave it no more than a single awed glance, before he turned in the other direction, hurrying toward the rear of the house.

He found a window, on the blind side of the building. It was locked and had been seldom opened. He struggled with the catch, then impatiently smashed it out with the butt of the rifle. He knocked out all the jagged splinters of glass and slipped through, dropping the short distance to the ground.

There was no action here; no one saw him. Keyed-up excitement pulled the lips back from his teeth as he started running.

More than once, climbing the barren hill behind the ranch, he slipped and fell in the dark. Rocks and brush tore at him; he was panting when he reached level ground. And here he turned, for a look at the scene he had left below.

The raid was over; the attackers had done their work and gone. He could see the Winship men—two or three shadowy figures who moved about the yard—looking like men dazed and stunned by catastrophe. The second fire, started by Keating himself, had helped seal the doom of the Spur house. It was a flaming pyre, sending red billows of smoke toward a high cloud ceiling that covered the stars. With the night wind whipping at it, there was only the question of how long it would take to be consumed.

He felt no touch of remorse, no sympathy for Matt Winship, who had spent so many years of his life building this ranch. Paul Keating had always hated the building, which had been a kind of prison for him since his marriage to Winship's stepdaughter. Now, its ashes would serve to bury all traces of his own guilt, and of the foolish trust that had led him to embezzlement. The books with their damning figures were gone; no one would ever know how much of

Winship's money had gone into the hands of a smooth-talking swindler, how much of it might have been taken from the safe by one of the perpetrators of tonight's raid.

New riders were pounding into the ranch yard—Spur crewmen, summoned by the torchflare of the burning house that must be visible for many miles. Keating scarcely noticed them. He was thinking of the money that weighted down his pockets. He must dispose of it somehow. Best to hide it, for the time being, somewhere right on this hill. Then, later recovered—and the thought filled him with sudden elation —it should be enough to buy him independence of this harsh country that he hated. A new start for himself and Fern, somewhere far from the shadow of Matt Winship.

Large slabs of rock crested the bare hill. At the foot of one of them he should find a temporary burial for the loot. He was busily searching when a sound made him freeze, to crouch motionless in shadow as two riders came walking their horses along the ridgetop. His hand tightened convulsively on the balance of the rifle.

The pair reined in, not a dozen yards from him, making a confused silhouette in the thin light. They must have been drawn by the reflection of fire that boiled at the sky. One spoke, and in astonishment he recognized the voice of his wife: "My God, Webb! What's happening down there?"

And Webb Toland's cool, cynical answer: "It should be obvious. Somebody's getting even for the loss of Ute Flats to that roughneck, Gary. I'd say it was Burl Hoffman's doings."

Paul Keating stared. Webb Toland! Here with Fern, when Keating would have supposed he was hours gone by now! His thoughts boggled as he began dimly to sense what this could mean.

He wasn't to be left long in doubt.

"Do you suppose," he heard his wife say, "anybody was hurt? What—what if Paul—"

Toland's sneering laugh jarred in Keating's ear. "Only wish we could count on it! If he could just get himself conveniently killed, it would make things all that much simpler for us!"

THE LURKING GUN

"Why, what a dreadful way to talk!" she exclaimed, but she didn't sound too shocked. And Toland laughed again.

"Come off it! You don't really care what happens to him. You've told me so yourself. It's me you're in love with!"

"Just the same—" But then the talk broke off and they both turned in their saddles, as Paul Keating strode toward them with the rifle braced against his hip.

"Damn you!" Keating's voice was a shaking, bleating scream. "At last I see you for what you are! You've made a fool of me at every step, Toland. You tricked me into embezzlement, and now you take my wife!"

Trembling hands lifted the rifle. But before he could work the trigger, the other man was already in motion. A gun leaped into Webb Toland's hand, glinted light as it slanted down across the saddle. It roared, with a flare of muzzle flash.

The rifle in Keating's hands went off in a wild and unaimed shot, and then the thrust of the explosion flung the weapon from his hands. He stumbled, going down with a great, exploding pressure tearing his chest apart. In his ears, his wife's startled scream mingled with the echoes of the guns.

IX

Jim Gary lifted a hand sharply, to cut off the tumble of excited words spilling from Ed Saxon's lips. "Hold it! he snapped. "Thought I heard more gunshots!"

The puncher's face twisted in concentration. "You're right! Sounded like up there on the hill!"

Promptly they kicked the spurs and sent their already lathered horses pounding across the yard, that was lighted eerily by the wind-whipped torch that had been Matt Winship's ranch house. Seasoned timbers had caught the flames readily, and though some of the Spur hands were rushing about in futile efforts to curb the fire or at least salvage something, Jim Gary had known with the first look that nothing could be done, other than keep the drifting brands from starting more fires.

Such pointless, wanton destruction had left Jim Gary stunned. He had thought Winship's enemies might have some further ideas of grabbing off strategic sections of graze, but he'd never imagined a guard was needed for the home ranch itself. Still, it had been his responsiblity and he blamed himself for this disaster. He was in a bad mood as he raced toward the rise of the hill, with Ed Saxon at his stirrup.

Their horses were blowing before they topped it. Gary pulled in, and his gun was in his hand as he hunted the shadows. After those two shots there had been nothing more, nor could he see anything moving here. But suddenly Ed Saxon grunted, "Yonder!" Someone was standing beside a horse. As they rode over, the figure raised its head and it was Fern Keating.

At the same moment Gary saw the man lying at her feet. She said, in an odd voice, "I—I just rode up and found him like this. I think he's dead."

Gary was already piling out of the saddle. Kneeling, he

saw at once that the man on the ground was Paul Keating. "Ed!" he ordered sharply. "Give me a light here."

The match that Saxon snapped alight on a thumbnail showed Keating's condition plainly. He was still breathing, but dark blood welling from the hole in his chest could mean only one thing. Knowing he had only moments, Gary seized the dying man by a shoulder and spoke his name.

The head rolled limply. The eyes wavered open and glinted oddly in the matchlight. Blood flecked his lips as Keating strained for breath.

"Keating!" Jim Gary demanded. "Who did this?"

A name struggled to frame itself on the slack lips, but there was no breath behind it. Blood ran thickly from a corner of the dying man's mouth.

"Can't you speak? Can you show me where he went?"

A hand was able to raise itself, feebly, and gesture into the surrounding darkness. Then it fell limp. The eyes wavered past Gary, to touch the face of the woman who bent close over the latter's shoulder. They came to a focus and Jim Gary saw in them a look of such utter revulsion as he had never seen. Keating appeared to be trying to draw away from her. The lips stirred again, wordlessly.

As he stared at the man, the match flickered and died. By the time Saxon had dug up another and got it burning, the moment was over. Paul Keating's eyes stared sightlessly. The labored breathing was still.

Ed Saxon swore as the second match burned his fingers. He shook it out, but the image of that last, hating look was imprinted on Jim Gary's mind as he got to his feet and turned to face the woman. "How did you happen to find your husband?"

"I was riding," she said. "Alone. I saw the reflection of the fire, and it made me head back across the hill."

"Then you didn't see the shooting?"

"No. I already told you—"

"Did you see anyone riding away? Or hear them?"

She shook her head—a little too quickly, he thought. "I didn't see or hear a thing."

Somehow he knew she was lying.

"I suppose he must have run up here to get away from the fighting," Fern went on. "It's just about what he'd have done."

An exclamation broke from Ed Saxon. "Jim! Would you look at this? What the hell you suppose he was doing with this much money in his pockets?" The puncher rose with what he had found: a double handful of greenbacks, held together by wide rubber bands, and a canvas sack that gave out the clink of coins. As Jim Gary looked at it, he had a sudden picture of the box safe in Winship's study—and, with it, a half-formed thought that he didn't like.

He asked the woman, "You know anything about it?"

"Why, no. Of course not! How would I?"

"Well, it'll have to wait. Get him down below," he told Saxon, "and take charge. Nothing much left to do down there, except try to keep that damned fire from spreading."

"We could take the fight to the skunks that started it!"

"Maybe later. Right now, my feeling is that it's more important I get on the trail of the one who got Keating."

"Not alone! You need someone with you."

"I can manage."

"But you'd be riding blind!" Ed Saxon pointed out. "And at night! You could run into an ambush. Jim, let me—"

It had been a long day, and his beaten body was too near exhaustion to give him patience. "You've got your orders! You're needed here."

There was no more argument. In strained silence they lifted Keating's body across the saddle of Saxon's horse, and Gary stood and watched the puncher lead it away down the slope. Afterward, alone with Fern Keating, he turned and faced her in the faint reflection from the burning house. Night wind blew its chill breath along the ridgetop, rattling dry grass and scrub growth as it rushed in toward the fire.

Gary said, "I'm wondering how much you really care. About losing him."

Her head jerked at his bluntness. But she showed no outrage. "I can't see," she retorted calmly, "what business it is of yours.

"None, I suppose," he admitted. "I never even really knew the man. But I saw the expression on his face as he was dying—his look when he saw you. If I were a woman, doesn't seem to me I'd want to remember hatred like that on my husband's face—"

She slapped him, a stinging blow. "You're contemptible!" she flared between set teeth. "Because my father hired you, I suppose you think it gives you a right to talk that way to me!"

"Nobody gave me the right," Jim Gary said. "I helped myself."

"While you're at it, why don't you just go ahead and say that I killed him?"

"I thought of that," he admitted. "But I don't really believe it. I don't think you're this good an actress! What I do know is that there's something going on here that I don't understand yet. And if it's of concern to Matt Winship, then I'm making it part of my job to dig it out."

Her face was a pale blur that he couldn't read, but he could see the rapid fall of her breath, hear the rasp of her breathing. "Don't be too sure!" Fern Keating told him harshly. "You were hired and you can be fired again. You may find out you're not as important to anyone here as you seem to think you are!"

In a flash she whirled, caught up the reins of her horse. She fumbled at the stirrup and lifted into saddle, as Jim Gary stood watching, with no move to help her mount. She gave him a last flickering glance, then swung her bridles with an angry wrench that made the horse toss its head.

She was gone then, flinging the horse at a reckless pace down the slope. Jim Gary let her go. He turned tiredly to

103

his own horse and swung astride, with more than this woman to occupy his attention.

He had nothing to go on but a vague gesture he thought he'd seen Keating's dying hand make. He pointed his horse in that direction, over the top of the ridge and away from what was left of the raided ranch. It stood to reason, anyway, that this was the course the killer would have had to take.

Riding blind, he let the animal carry him into the head of a shallow gully that deepened as it funneled down off the ridge. Loose rubble skittered past him. Wind rattled the heads of dry brush that cloaked this face of the ridge. But where the earth leveled off, he swung down and fished up a match which he scraped alight upon a spur rowel.

Almost at once, he saw what he hoped for. It was the distinct, freshly printed mark of a shod hoof. Casting ahead, he found another before the match died and left him momentarily blinded. Another rider had used this route, only minutes before him, and the horse had been traveling with a widespaced, reaching stride.

Quickly Gary remounted and took up the chase, knowing all the odds were against him. The killer had too good a lead for night hunting. Besides, he would know the country and Gary did not. But the circumstances of Paul Keating's death were so tangled with the other problems of this range that he wasn't going to give up the chase without at least a token effort.

A dry ravine seemed to open into a notch in the next low ridge, and he took it, using the spur and trusting the horse to find good footing. The ground was sandy and muffled the thud of hoofs. Once he reined in to use another match. The bottom of the ravine was often used by cattle and was pocked with their sign, but he thought he saw fresh hoofprints.

He kept going, coming up out of the ravine and across the flinty comb of the succeeding ridge. Beyond lay sagebrush and a dark line that looked like willows following a dry watercourse. Gary reined in briefly, and as he did the wind blowing against his face brought him the brief and sudden rattle of hoofs crossing rock, somewhere distantly ahead. That spurred him, and turned him reckless. He came down off the low ridge at a full gallop. Tall sage whipped against his legs as he drove the horse through it, and its pungent odor surrounded him.

And then, as the willows swept blackly nearer, muzzle flame lashed out of their shadow. He heard the snap of the rifle, even as he felt the horse start to stumble under him. By instinct he kicked free of the stirrups. The skewbald, having taken the bullet in midstride, tripped and went down in a complete somersault, and Gary sailed across its rump and narrowly missed the flying steel of its rear hoofs.

He was able to loosen his body and hit the ground limply, but he felt for a moment as though all the life had been slammed out of him.

The rifle in the willows flatted off a second time, but this shot flew wild. It alerted Gary, however. With the night still spinning around him, he groped for his holster and his fingers closed on empty leather. The gun had dropped out in his fall. Alarmed, he started up to his knees. Pain shot through him. He found himself dropping weakly forward, and when he put out a hand to catch himself his palm touched metal. It was the barrel of his own gun!

Fumbling, he grabbed it up and then he was moving crabwise, in a scramble for the protection of his dead mount. Even as he did so, a third bullet chewed up the dirt, just inches from him.

Jim Gary flattened himself and triggered twice across the warm barrel of the horse, paused, and fired again. He had to duck as a bullet came screaming low above his head, but instantly he raised himself and shot twice, directly at the smearing after-image of the muzzle flash. An unlearned instinct that kept count of the shots told him, then, his gun was empty. Without triggering on a spent shell, he dropped back and proceeded to reload.

He was feeling sickly dizzy from the pain in his chest; the

earth seemed to rock beneath him, and he felt the cold sweat on his face. The hand that thumbed fresh shells from his belt loops dropped them into the dirt. Panting, he paused to slide a hand in under his shirt and test the bandage, but he could find no warmth of blood. The wound in his chest hadn't reopened, at least.

Then he had the gun refilled and he rocked the cylinder into place, turning back to his hidden enemy. It occurred to him that minutes had passed since there had been any sound from the willow thicket. Perhaps one of his blind shots had been lucky. On the other hand, the ambusher could be waiting for him to be fooled into exposing himself for a better target.

Impatience had its way. After a long count of twenty he brought his feet under him and came cautiously to a stand, the reloaded gun leveled and ready. Still nothing, there in the shadows.

Then he heard a rider coming—but from behind! He whirled, to seek this new danger. Moonlight filtered by the high overcast showed him the horseman picking his way through the thick sagebrush, and he placed his gun on the figure and his finger took up triggerslack.

The rider halted. Hack Bales's voice sounded across the stillness: "Gary! You there?"

He eased the tension out of him, lowering the gun as he called answer. The puncher rode quickly up, reining in as he saw the other man standing beside a dead horse. "Saxon told me to come after you," he said. "What's happening here, anyway?"

Gary gave him a quick explanation. "Whoever he is, I'm sure he's the one that murdered Keating. I've either plugged him, or he's pulled out."

"We'll soon see which!"

Ignoring Gary's warning to caution, Hack Bales circled the dead horse and spurred straight toward the trees. Gary stood with the night wind blowing against him, straining for a sound and hearing only the noise the Spur rider made as he crashed through the dry branches. For a long moment there was dead silence.

At last he saw Hack Bales returning. The man rode up and reported briefly, "Got away. Did you get a look at him?"

"No. Maybe, in the morning—"

Hack Bales shook his head. "You'll never pick up a trail. Not in those flint hills! If there'd ever been rustlers in this country, they could have stripped the range clean and not much anyone could of done about it. Only luck for us they never tried!" He added anxiously, "Hey! Are you hurt, Gary?"

He must have seen something in the other's manner that alarmed him but though he was still shaky from the fall he'd taken, Gary shook his head. As he turned to strip the saddle off the dead horse, he said, "What about the ranch?"

"The house is still burning. We couldn't save it. Johnson says it was Burl Hoffman and his crowd, all right. He got a good look at some of them during the raid."

"They're a bunch of mad dogs!" Gary said grimly. "No more casualties, I hope? Aside from Keating?"

Bales didn't answer during the moment it took him to accept the heavy stock saddle and swing it up in front of him. Reluctantly he answered, "One more I'm afraid."

About to step into the stirrup Bales had cleared for him, Gary paused and looked at him sharply. "Who?"

The answer was heavy with anger. "We found Pete Dunn afterward. We figure he must have tried to get off his bunk and take a hand in the fighting. Bad hurt as he was, it was just too much. . . ."

There was nothing to say. Face grim, Jim Gary pulled himself with a painful effort to a place behind Hack Bales. Silently, the horse with its double burden started back for the raided ranch.

All that remained of the house, by now, was a pile of charred timbers and stone, and glowing coals that leaped to blue flame when the ground wind breathed upon them.

False dawn stained the eastern sky as the Spur crew, gray with fatigue and soot-grimed, gathered in the kitchen for coffee and a grim discussion. Sound of an approaching wagon sent someone to the door, and then the shout went up: "Hey! It's Matt! It's the Old Man!"

Quickly, Jim Gary strode outside and, with the rest of the crew, watched the rig and team pull into the yard. On the seat, Matt Winship stared around him with a bleak expression. Tracy Bannister, in a heavy coat and with a shawl knotted about her head, handled the team. It was only when he saw Fern Keating, following the wagon on her horse, that Gary realized how Winship must have learned the news of disaster.

"He made me bring him," Tracy said quickly, as she kicked on the brake. "She came and told him what had happened, and he insisted." Gary saw tears on her cheeks as she looked at the ruin of the house. "Oh, how terrible! And—and is it true, about poor Pete Dunn?"

"I'm afraid so."

Matt Winship stirred, but he made no move to step down yet. His bearded face, in the sickly dawn light, was ashen, lined with bitterness and shock. He sought Jim Gary and his eyes settled sternly on the man. He said, in his deep rumble of a voice, "Gary, I hold you responsible for this!"

The words were like a blow. Gary heard the small stir they made, among the crewmen grouped about the wagon.

Tracy cried indignantly, "Matt! You know that isn't fair! They pulled this raid in retaliation."

"Yes!" he retorted. "Retaliation for the fight he took it on himself to stage at Ute Flats. I gave him no such authority!"

"Would you rather he'd stood by and let them grab whatever they wanted, without lifting a finger?"

"Then at least," the old man answered, "Pete Dunn would still be alive! Rather that, a thousand times, than try to hold onto a few acres of open range that never really belonged to me, and that I'm not going to need much longer, in any event!

"It's a good thing," he went on doggedly, "that my daughter forced her way into my room and made me see what kind of thing's been going on. Plain to see nobody else would have told me." His gaze settled on Jim Gary. "Any more than you would have told me you disobeyed my plain instructions about sending that wire of acceptance to Chicago!"

"When it comes to that," Gary said flatly, "you knew the kind of man I was when you hired me. You must have guessed that if Hoffman and that crowd threw me a challenge, I wasn't the one to walk away from it!

"I'm sorry as hell about Pete Dunn. But he was another man who preferred to fight." He lifted his shoulders, let them fall. "Still, you're the boss. If you say so, then I did wrong. I can still send that telegram."

"No need to bother," Matt Winship said. "You're fired!"

Gary couldn't believe it. "Are you serious?"

"Since you won't do the job I hired you for, I'll pay you your time, and then manage the job myself!"

There was a silence. Jim Gary drew a long breath. He ran a glance over the faces around him, saw the same stunned look on all of them.

On all but one. Fern Keating returned his stare with a look of triumph, and he knew suddenly that this was exactly what she had hoped to accomplish by running to her stepfather with this news of disaster—without bothering to care how the shock of it might affect him.

Tracy Bannister's voice shook with hurt and anger. "Matt, I'm ashamed of you! Really ashamed! You knew he never wanted this job. He only took it as a favor. No other man would have troubled to do what he's tried to—"

"Let it go, Tracy." Jim Gary shook his head tiredly. "Thanks, but let it go. I'll be leaving." He started to turn, then paused. "Forget about the pay," he told Winship. "I'll take it out in the loan of a horse to get me into town. I'll leave him at the stable."

He walked toward the corral, a tall, weary shape of a man

whose face showed the aches in his tired body, the harsher hurts that roiled his spirit. As they watched him go, the raw, burnt stink of the gutted house tanged the chill mists of dawn.

X

BURL HOFFMAN's home ranch was a bachelor layout, the main house being a mere tar-paper shack where he lived with his crew; he was apparently a man with no need for either solitude or privacy. The morning after the raid and fire at Spur, the yard filled early with saddle horses. By prior arrangement, the ranchers who had pooled their interests in opposing Matt Winship and the syndicate sale were gathering for a council of war.

A glum mood lay on all of them, though there was some good news, at least, as a result of last night's grim doings. Jim Gary had been fired, for one thing. No one seemed to know for sure whether he had already left the country, or perhaps was in town somewhere. But George Ruby, someone said, had unpinned his sheriff's badge and laid it on the desk in the dusty jail building and got on his horse and ridden out of Antler for good, rather than face the risks of trying to deal with a worsening situation. It meant that for the time being they had a free hand.

But if there was reason for satisfaction, it was strangely muted. News of the death of old Pete Dunn rested heavily on all these men, like the pall of smoke that hung in the motionless upper air over Spur headquarters. They had all known and respected the old cowpuncher. There wasn't a one who didn't regret what had happened, or wouldn't have avoided it if he could.

Filing into the house, they saw with some surprise the man who sat at ease in a chair by the oilcloth-covered table smoking a slim cigar and evidently waiting for the meeting to begin. Old Priday Jones stopped dead and, scowling, demanded of their host, "What's *he* doing here?"

Burl Hoffman felt himself on the defensive, after last night. "Webb Toland's our friend," he said. "He sees our side of this fight, and he's been telling me some ideas he has for helping us win it."

111

"That don't make sense," Jones retorted. Someone else said, with suspicion, "Yah! Why should he stick his neck out when it's none of it any of his business?"

If Toland sensed hostility, he didn't show it. He coolly tapped ash from his cigar and answered the questions himself, before the sandy-haired leader had time to frame a reply.

"Don't make any mistakes," the mining man said, his whole manner unruffled. "I've got no more love for a syndicate than the rest of you. And with good reason. I've seen how they operate! They get in here with cattle, and sooner or later they're going to hear what I've been doing at the Copper Queen. Next thing, they'll be wanting to cut in for themselves. With their money, they can beat me out of some valuable properties I've got my eye on. I have no intention of letting that happen!"

"There you are!" said Burl Hoffman, eyeing the silent group. "You all ready to admit you yelped a little soon? You willing now to listen to what Mr. Toland is offering?"

Except perhaps for old Priday Jones, to whom this outsider had always appeared too well-dressed, too well-spoken, they had all tended to be impressed by Toland's facade as a successful and resourceful man. Their hostility melted and now Vince Alcord said, "I'm never too proud to accept help from any source, when I'm in the middle of a fight!"

"Good enough!" Hoffman was pleased as he saw the change of attitude. "As I say, I've been listening to Mr. Toland's ideas and I think they answer our problem. But you've got to decide. I'll go along with whatever the rest of you say."

And so Webb Toland took the floor, and he chose his words carefully.

"I think you're set on the right track," he told them. "What you've got to do is create a situation to convince the syndicate bigwigs that buying in Spur will cost more in the way of trouble than it's worth. Burning out the ranch last night— that was a good move, because it shows you're in dead earnest. And if Matt Winship gets hurt, or loses a man or two . . . well, he started this; *you* didn't ask for the fight. But you've got too much at stake to pull your punches!"

Heads were lifting among the listeners. Shoulders straightened and jaws set, as Toland cleverly helped them justify the very things some had begun to regret. He sensed this and smiled inwardly, knowing that now he could count on their complete support.

"This morning, I happen to know, Winship sent off a rider to the telegraph office at Elko, with a wire accepting the syndicate's offer. They'll undoubtedly have their men here within a week. Before then, you'll have to strike, and strike hard. The sooner the better."

"Where?" Vince Alcord demanded. "If you think you know the answer, spell it out for us."

"I'm thinking there's one move that would cinch matters—create a situation no Eastern outfit would even consider touching." He paused for effect. "Just suppose," he said slowly, "that Spur was all at once to begin losing stock."

This caused a stir of shocked reaction. Priday Jones cried hoarsely, "You—you ain't trying to suggest we turn cattle thieves?"

"I'm suggesting it's no time for half-measures," Toland replied firmly. "The setup for rustling is perfect, here. In the hills east of Spur, a trail can be lost beyond any chance of finding it." He might have added that he had just finished proving this himself. He wondered if that arrogant rough-neck, Jim Gary, had wasted any more time trying to pick up sign on the man who ambushed him from the willows last night.

He went on: "I can think of no better beginning than the special herd of Black Angus stock Winship's holding on that graze under Buck Ridge. It's a valuable bunch of stock, and being that close to the hills, it makes a natural target. The syndicate will really be impressed!"

"Maybe." But Vince Alcord, frowning, was troubled. "I ain't saying you're wrong; I'm near ready to tackle anything that might settle this matter. But Winship sets a lot of store by that damned herd of his. It won't be taken without a fight. And what happens if some of us are recognized?"

"You won't be," Toland assured him. "Naturally, I thought of that. And it's the place where I come in.

"Up at the Queen, I've got some men on my payroll that I'll be glad to make available for this job. They're good men— I hire them to guard my property and my interests, and I pay them enough that they follow orders. What's more, they're not the kind to lose their heads if some Spur rider should empty a cartridge or two at them. It's true, of course, they know nothing much about handling cattle, but that's your department. The beauty of it is that even if they're seen none of their faces are known here on Antler range."

"So?" Alcord still didn't catch the drift of his thought.

"So we work together. My boys will go in first and take care of any guard. And when that's done, some of you will be standing by to move in and help yourselves to the beef. It's as simple as that."

Alcord's eyes narrowed. "And how about you? You going to be taking any personal part in all this? Any of the risk?"

"Naturally," Toland answered curtly. "I'll be there." His part was a feature he meant to keep to himself. If these fools could guess even a little of what was working in his crafty mind, they would have been in for a shock. Triumph tugged slightly at a corner of his mouth, as he saw them rising to the bait he had carefully spread for them.

"It's entirely up to you," he finished, prodding for a decision. "If it's too risky for you, say so. There's other ways I can protect my interests. But let me say this: Once a syndicate *does* move in on you, you'll find them a lot harder neighbor to deal with than Matt Winship ever was!"

Burl Hoffman said loudly, "I'm convinced! I vote to go along with Webb Toland, and waste no time about it! What do the rest of you say?"

They said it, in a general chorus of agreement. Webb Toland's keen eye discovered only one holdout. Old Priday

Jones, scowling to himself in a corner of the room, didn't like any part of what was happening here.

If he had the rest, then the hell with Priday Jones! The old bastard could be silenced if he tried to make trouble. Toland listened to the noisy outbreak of voices eagerly discussing the plan that had been adopted. It was always an immense pleasure, to see how he could lead fools to his wishes, to see the parts of a well-laid plan dropping smoothly into place.

Tracy Bannister, sorting mail behind the desk, looked up at a step and a shadow in the doorway. When she saw who had entered, her eyes darkened and she quietly put down the letters she was holding. Not speaking, she waited.

Despite her emotion, she had to admit that Fern Keating had never looked more beautiful or self-assured than she did this afternoon, in divided skirt and whipcord packet. Her blouse had a bunch of frilly material at the throat, and a pert riding hat sat perfectly upon her gleaming hair. In one hand she carried a leather riding crop which she slapped against the other palm, as she looked with superior aloofness about the cramped and ill-furnished hotel lobby, and then let her glance settle on the girl behind the desk.

Without a word of greeting she walked forward, and from her pocket she drew out a couple of bills and tossed them down in front of Tracy.

"What's this?" Tracy demanded coldly.

"Payment for the room my father used. Does that cover it?"

"Are you trying to make a joke? You know I'd never charge Matt Winship room rent, no matter how long he stayed!"

"I'm paying for the room," Fern repeated crisply. "So there'll be no obligations left unsettled. And after that I want you to stay away from him, and from Spur. I think you have entirely too much influence over my father!"

For a moment Tracy could not believe what she'd heard. But what she read in those eyes turned her cold with understanding. She said, icily calm, "I owe more to Matt Winship than to any man I ever knew, outside of my own father. If I

115

can ever help him, in return, I'll always do it. And there's no way you can stop me."

"I think there are ways," Fern answered. "I've heard talk around town—nasty, childish talk, about you and Matt Winship. If you were to cross me, I could make plenty of people believe those rumors aren't so entirely childish!"

Tracy Bannister stared, incredulous at such a threat. Suddenly she couldn't refrain herself. She heard herself calling Fern Keating a name—an unladylike word she had never thought would cross her lips. The other woman's breast lifted on a quickly drawn breath. Next moment, the leather whip in her hand was raised and came slashing squarely at Tracy's cheek.

Moving too quickly for her, Tracy caught the blow against her forearm. Then she seized Fern's wrist, wrested the riding crop from her, and flung it angrily across the lobby. She said tensely, "I'd just like to know what your really after! You deliberately maneuvered to have Jim Gary fired. Now you want me to stay away from Matt because you know I have his interests at heart, and that he listens to me. Why? He's almost your own father. Do you really want him to lose the ranch that means so much to him?"

Fern Keating jerked her arm free. She stood rubbing the wrist that was red from the grip of Tracy's fingers, her eyes flaming with fury and hatred for the girl across the desk. But what she might have said went unspoken, for a sudden anguished voice pulled them both quickly around, toward the sun-filled doorway.

"Miz Keating!"

It looked like an apparition that came lurching through the door, his shoulder striking the edge of the frame and throwing him off stride. But it was only old Priday Jones, clothing awry and white hair streaming into his face. "Miz Keating!" he said again, hollowly, and set a weaving course across the linoleum flooring. He put a hand on the desk and leaned heavily, peering at Matt Winship's daughter.

"You're drunk!" she said in disgust.

"Yes, ma'am. If I wasn't, I wouldn't be here! It's tooken me all day to find the nerve to do what I know I have to. Then, when I seen your bronc tied at the pole outside—"

Alarmed, the quarrel of a moment ago forgotten now, Tracy seized the old rancher by a trembling arm. "What is it, Priday? What is it you're trying to tell us?"

"That I don't hold with rustling, even if it means turning against my own kind! Oh, I told 'em I wouldn't go along, but that ain't enough! I got to stop it! I got to tell—"

"Tell what?" she insisted. "Stop them from what, Priday?"

Then it came out, the whole sordid story of the scene at Hoffman's, and the program Webb Toland had sold the men who met there. "Reckon maybe I'm a traitor," he finished despondently. "But, by God, there's some things a man just can't hold still for!"

Jim Gary spoke from the lobby stairs. "You did right," he said. "Don't blame yourself, if your conscience said it had to be done."

They hadn't seen him there, listening to the old man's troubled story. Now he came down to the lobby, carrying his bedroll and the saddle Tracy Bannister had recovered from the bushes at the stageline corral. He set them down near the doorway, and turned to Jones. "When's this business supposed to take place?"

"This very afternoon," the old man answered miserably. "They ain't lettin' any grass grow under their boots. May be too late already to do anything."

"And it may not!" Gary turned to Fern. "You'd better get started for Spur as fast as you can ride! Let them know what we've learned. Tell them Webb Toland's gone and got himself mixed up in it now, for some reason we don't yet know. And get the crew burning leather for Buck Ridge! Meanwhile I'll head directly out there to see if there's anything I can do."

Fern Keating only looked at him, as though she hadn't understood. Impatiently, he took her by an arm and pushed her toward the door. "Didn't you hear? There's no time to lose! Get on that horse of yours and try to act as though you had some stake in what happens to your father's ranch!"

She didn't argue. She gave him one hate-filled stare, and then she pulled away from his hands and hurried out of the hotel and down the steps to her waiting horse. She mounted and quickly left town, heading north.

But with the town behind her she pulled rein and sat a moment, debating. Directly ahead lay the road to Spur, where there were the riders Jim Gary would be counting on to help save Matt Winship's precious Black Angus holding.

She gave that road no more than a glance. Instead, she pulled out of the trail and then was cutting north and east toward a higher fording of Antler Creek, and a short route to Buck Ridge.

If Priday Jones had told the truth, Webb Toland would be there. Her lover must be warned that his plans had been betrayed, and that he was in danger.

Jim Gary and the girl watched old Priday Jones peg away into the glare of the sunlight. Tracy shook her head. "I'm so sorry for him!" she exclaimed. "It must have been a terrible decision!"

"I don't think he'd ever have forgiven himself if he hadn't made it." A need for action turned Gary back into the lobby then. He had slept and was feeling fresh. The wound in his chest was no more than a dull ache as he leaned to take up his saddle and blanket roll. When he straightened, the girl was standing before him.

"You're going out there? Alone?" She shook her head. "Even after all that's happened, you still mean to fight Matt Winship's battles. After he threw your help back in your face? No one would expect it, Jim. Not when you could just ride on out of this country and forget its problems. They're not yours."

He shrugged. "A man doesn't always have a reason for what he does. When he's once picked up a problem, even for a day or two, it sometimes isn't easy to lay it down again. How do you know? Maybe I resent having a horse shot out from under me. Or maybe it's just that I'm curious to know what that smooth-talking Webb Toland has in his head. Maybe it's no more than that."

Tracy shook her head. "All the talking in the world won't make me believe you're anything but what I've known you were: a very fine and very unselfish man!" And then, without warning, she came up onto her toes and her warm mouth pressed against his.

Gary was taken utterly by surprise. He stood with arms loaded down by his possessions, and before he could move to drop them the kiss was over and she was stepping back, fast, a mingled sweetness and confusion in her face. He stood and stared at her like a fool. And then, because there was nothing to say, he turned and walked out of the building.

The softness of her kiss was still on his lips and his mind was a maze of bewildered thoughts as, moments later, he stood in the gloom of the public livery stable, fastening his saddle on the back of the horse he'd ridden in from Spur this morning, after being fired. Whatever had possessed her? he asked himself, and got no answer. Yet he knew that nothing in his experience had ever changed the shape of his world so completely. You couldn't just ride away from a thing like *that*. Once this business at Buck Ridge was settled, one way or another. . . .

Still, who and what was he—with his dubious past and uncertain future—to make too much of what could have been a mere impetuous gesture, that the girl perhaps already regretted?

So filled was he with these thoughts that, as he finished saddling and took the reins to lead his horse from its stall, he scarcely noticed the two men who stood waiting in the gloom near the double doors. Not until the bigger one spoke to him in the unforgotten voice of Boyd Plank: "All right, Gary. It's been a long chase you led us, but we finally run you down. Now, stand and take it!"

XI

THEIR guns were in the holsters, he saw. But their hands were tight upon the grips. Caught flat-footed, Gary could make no move toward his own weapon. He said heavily, "So you found me."

"We come near never doin' it," big Boyd Plank told him. "We was halfway to Arizona before we knew for sure we'd tooken a wrong trail."

"It was the bronc you left in the corral that fooled us," his slighter, younger brother Asa explained. "We thought sure, when we seen it there that night, you must have roped you a fresh mount and pushed on." He frowned, a man darkly puzzled. "But I just don't get it! You've had three days, now, when you could have been losing us for good. Why are you still here?"

Jim Gary, thinking of all that had happened, said a little bitterly, "I wonder the same damned thing!"

A horse stomped in one of the stalls. High in a corner of the rafters, a couple of hornets hummed about their mud-daub nest.

Asa said, "It's your move, Gary!"

Gary's chest felt cramped. The pressures on him were roweling him hard, and even though his life hung on the trigger fingers of this vengeful pair, they could be no more than a distraction. He took a deep breath. "Now, listen—" he began.

"Listen, hell!" Boyd Plank snapped. "We ain't letting ourselves be slick-talked! We got a score to settle. There's a gun in your holster. Pull it!"

"Against the two of you? You call that fair odds?"

"It's as fair odds as a trained gunfighter goading a youngster like Lane into the draw!"

Gary's mouth pulled down hard. "I never goaded your brother!" he started to answer, but then the hopelessness of it all quieted him. "All right, skip that! I know you'd never in a million years believe my side of the story!

"You've caught me, and I suppose you'll do what you want. Just the same, there's something I've got to ask you to let me do first, a job that's waiting. If I can have just two hours—"

"Two hours for what?" snapped Asa. "A head start?"

"You ain't going nowhere!" Boyd Plank told him. "You're not getting away from us a second time!"

They were implacable, beyond reasoning. A kind of despair touched Jim Gary as he felt the moments tick by. His hand moved nearer the jutting handle of his gun, tempted to drag it out and make a showdown. "I won't try to escape," he promised hoarsely. "My word of honor on that."

Asa Plank sneered and his scorn was like a blow across the face. "The honor of a hired gunman?"

"Mister," Boyd Plank said, "we wouldn't take your word for nothing!"

"I'm afraid you're going to have to!" Tracy Bannister said, behind him.

She was a little breathless, and white of face, but she was determined, and the shotgun she held braced against a hip was steady enough. The Planks stiffened, and very slowly they turned. When they saw the weapon's shining tube, and the girl's hand white-knuckled on the trigger guard, they reacted visibly. Slowly, without bidding, they raised their hands.

Asa said, "Now, lady—"

"Get their guns, Jim!" she said. "And please hurry! This thing makes me nervous!"

Quickly he stepped forward and took the sixshooters from the brothers' holsters, dropping them into the straw of a manger. "I think they'll be good now," he said. "Thanks, Tracy."

She eased her grip on the shotgun, but she kept it ready. "They came in the hotel," she answered his unvoiced question, "checking the desk register. I knew who they must be, the minute I saw them."

"Can you hold them here a little longer?"

"I'll hold them!"

Jim Gary turned and swung into the saddle. He looked down at the scowling brothers. "I made you a promise," he said earnestly. "And I'll keep it. I'm not running again. I can see you'd find me eventually. I want this settled, but you've got to wait till my other business is finished."

Their faces were hate-filled, uncompromising, unbelieving. Seeing he would get no answer, Jim Gary kicked his horse and rode from the stable, ducking to clear the low doorway. Straightening, he let the bronc out, and used the spurs.

Webb Toland, standing beside his horse, watched Vince Alcord ride away through the scrub growth of Buck Ridge—a formation so-called because someone had once said its silhouette resembled that of a sleeping Paiute warrior. Toland's mouth quirked and he said, contemptuously, "Sucker!"

St. Cloud laughed shortly. He was a lath-lean shape of a man, who affected black clothing that made his face appear sallow and accented the shadows of his gaunt cheeks. His eyes, also black, glinted as coldly as chips of obsidian. With black-gloved hands, he settled the heavy shellbelt about his hips, checked the lashing of the tong that strapped the cutaway holster carefully in place.

He had done many jobs for Webb Toland, in the past, and between these two there was a complete meeting of minds. He said now, with cruel amusement, "The stupid bastard will never know what hit him."

. This ridge, and the lower one beyond, formed a sheltered draw that was ideal grazing for Matt Winship's prized herd; once the pair of riders who guarded it had been disposed of, that trough down there would serve equally well as a funnel to pour the herd straight into the flinty hills eastward. Just now Vince Alcord had ridden up to inform Toland that he and Burl Hoffman and their men were in position, ready to pick up the beef as soon as it could be started moving in their direction.

St. Cloud slanted a look at the sun, and then at the three

other men who waited, a little distance off, for instructions. He said, "About time to start this ball?"

"I told Alcord five minutes," Webb Toland answered. "There's no great hurry." And then both men turned, instantly alert, as they caught sound of a horse and rider approaching along the comb of the ridge, breaking through the scrub growth.

St. Cloud swore and the gun was in his hand in a sudden, effortless swipe of motion. But his boss told him sharply, "Put it away!" and was hurrying to meet Fern Keating when she rode up and dropped quickly from the saddle.

"What are you doing here?" he demanded.

She showed the effects of her breathless ride from town. She'd lost her pert riding hat and her beautiful auburn hair had come down in a wind-blown tangle. Her eyes blazed with shock and anger. "I came to find out if it was true—and I guess it is!"

"Don't talk in riddles! If what was true?"

"That you've joined Spur's enemies!" And she poured out what she had learned from Priday Jones in the hotel lobby. As she talked, Webb Toland's handsome face seemed to settle into hardness, his tawny eyes took on danger.

"So Jones talked!" he said quietly. "I didn't think he'd have the nerve!"

"Then you admit it's so?"

"Of course not!" He took her by the shoulders. She tried to shrug his hands away but he wouldn't free her. He spoke levelly, earnestly.

"Have you forgotten what I said about letting Hoffman and Alcord and the rest of those fools break themselves, and then picking up the pieces? That's exactly what I'm working on. Only I saw an opportunity to give things a little push!"

"How? By helping them steal our stock?"

"Will you be quiet a minute and let me explain?" He drew a long breath, summoning the patience he needed. "We only get the cattle started for them. Then they take over. I've already convinced them my boys aren't experienced in handling beef, which isn't exactly the truth."

"And then?"

"Well, naturally—being law-abiding citizens, who believe in justice and order—if we should see someone in the act of driving Spur cattle into the hills, we'd be expected to stop them. Any way we can."

She said, aghast, "I think you mean to wait for them somewhere and ambush them!"

"Why not? They're the ringleaders. With those two out of the way, the opposition to Spur collapses like a punctured balloon!"

"But the rest, who were at the meeting this morning, will know exactly what you've done! So will Jim Gary, and that Bannister girl!"

He shrugged. "Let them go to court and prove it! I can produce witnesses of my own to give iron-clad testimony that I couldn't possibly have been at their damned meeting." A smile tilted his mouth. "In a thing like this, a little cool bluff will beat an implausible truth, any time!"

"You may need more than bluff against Jim Gary! When I left he was all ready to take the saddle to stop you."

"Alone?" The name of Gary had caused Toland's face to darken slightly. "He must be crazy!"

"He has his share of cool nerve, too," she reminded him. "He thought I was riding to Spur to alert the crew. Instead, I came straight here."

"Then that means he's expecting help that won't be coming!" Toland nodded, satisfied, and made his quick decision. "It changes nothing. We'll proceed as planned, except that we'll leave a man posted, to watch for friend Gary and take care of him when he shows!"

He turned away, quickly giving his orders. One of St. Cloud's men pulled a saddle gun and checked the loads, and went looking for a spot to keep his watch for Gary. Toland was gathering the reins of his horse when St. Cloud came to

him, carrying a rifle. With it, the gunman indicated the
draw at the foot of the ridge.

"I might be able to pick off those guards from here," he
said. "It's not an impossible shot."

Toland's eyes narrowed as he considered. The two Spur
riders had a fire going, near a shallow bay of rocks near the
farther ridge. They were over there now, heating up a pot of
coffee. Toland gauged the distance, then reluctantly shook
his head.

"You could miss, too," he said. "And then they'd be into
those rocks and we'd have to dig them out. No, we'll ride
down. They know me; they'll not think anything suspicious,
before we're close enough to make damned sure of our shots."

Fern Keating couldn't hold back the exclamation: "You're
not going to ambush those men, too? My father's own
punchers?"

"What's the lives of a couple of illiterate cowhands, against
saving Spur?"

She was looking at him as though she had never quite seen
him clearly before this moment. "Is it your method to murder
every man who happens to get in your way? The way you
did Paul?"

"That wasn't murder!" Webb Toland said sharply, his eyes
cold. "The fool came at me with a gun. I had to protect
myself."

"You killed him because he was in your way," she repeated. "And how can I be sure that next time it might not
be my father? Or—" She shuddered, as the idea touched her
like a cold wind. "Or—even *me*?"

For a long moment his eyes rested on her, and they were
the eyes of a stranger. She faced him, a woman waiting for
an answer, for some assurance, something she could hold to
and believe. But Webb Toland was canny enough to see that
there was nothing worth saying. He wasted neither time nor
breath.

He turned abruptly, toed the stirrup and swung astride. St.

THE LURKING GUN

Cloud fell in beside him. With the two others trailing, they dropped slowly down the slope.

The two Spur crewmen were Hack Bales and the towhead, Cliff Frazer. As Webb Toland predicted, they recognized him at once and, seeing in him a successful businessman who was well respected by the people of this section, took no alarm at having him ride up on them. They straightened, leaving the coffee pot sitting in its bed of coals. As the newcomers reined up Hack Bales nodded greeting.

"Howdy," he said. "You're in time for a bait of java, if you don't mind that we only got two cups."

Webb Toland shook his head and piled both hands on the saddlehorn. Beyond the little fire, the black cattle herd grazed peacefully. A three-stand fence of barbed wire, snaking across the draw, cut it in two and held the beef in a grassy pocket that headed up where Buck Ridge joined its lower neighbor. A single-panel gate, now closed, would free the herd and let it be driven into the waiting hands of Alcord and Hoffman and their crews.

"No, thanks," said Toland. "We're not here to drink up your coffee. I heard somewhere you had a fire and a killing at Spur last night. Wondered if it was a fact."

"Your hearing's good, Mr. Toland!" young Cliff Frazer answered grimly. "They burnt the house and they same as murdered Pete Dunn."

"Mr. Keating, too," Hack Bales added.

Toland showed them a look of shock. "Keating? I hadn't heard that!"

"Shot him dead. No knowing what they'll try next. That's why we're doubling the guard, here and any other place they might take a mind to hit." The coffee on the fire suddenly came to a boil. Brown liquid fountained sluggishly from the spout as Hack Bales swore and leaped to snatch the pot from the coals. "Reckon this is hot as we need it," he said. "Sure you won't have a shot with us?"

126

Toland hesitated. Then he said quietly, "Why, sure. Why not?"

As Hack Bales turned to take the tin cup Cliff Frazer handed him, Toland's fingers closed around the butt of his gun. His eyes on the puncher's back, choosing a target, he heard the slight whisper of gunmetal against leather and knew St. Cloud was clearing a weapon.

"Hack! Cliff!" It was Jim Gary's sudden shout, breaking across the stillness. "It's a trick! *Look out!*"

Surprise stayed Toland's hand. Whipping around, he saw Gary on a lathered horse, spurring down the ravine where the two ridges headed up. Fury locked his jaw muscles tight, brought the gun out of its holster.

Where the hell was that guard he'd posted?

"They're after the herd!" Gary was shouting. His drawn gun winked reflected sunlight. But now, above and to his right, Toland's gunman came belatedly into view, rifle snapping to his shoulder. As flame and white smoke sprang from the muzzle, the bronc under Jim Gary squealed and then man and mount piled up in a wild, rolling tangle.

The horse pawed and struggled quickly to its feet, and with reins flying came sliding on down the trough, raising a huge boil of dust. And as this thinned and settled it became clear that Gary, too, had survived the spill. Was he indestructible?

Webb Toland swore, brought up his sixshooter and fired. At the same instant, St. Cloud or one of the others triggered also. It seemed to explode almost in Toland's ear, and it startled him and spoiled his own aim. With his whole head ringing he saw Gary take cover, safe, behind a half-buried boulder.

Furious, he turned back to the two Spur crewmen. Hack Bales stood like a man dumbstruck, the coffee pot still in his hand. Deliberately Toland fired and saw him spun and knocked off his feet as a bullet drilled his thigh.

That jarred Cliff Frazer into action. As Toland was leveling for a second, finishing shot, the young towhead gave a cry and grabbed wildly for the gun in his own holster. He jerked it out and emptied it blindly into the group of mounted men.

A bullet stung Toland's horse and brought the animal up rearing, to slam sidewards into St. Cloud's mount. For that moment all the horses were out of control and the riders had their hands full trying to settle them. And this was time enough for Cliff Frazer to get to his hurt companion, slip an arm under his shoulders, and start frantically dragging him toward the jumble of rocks just behind them.

Cursing his roan to a stand, Webb Toland looked for them, just in time to see them disappear into cover. He gripped his weapon in a fist that shook with impotent rage, as he saw how this Jim Gary had blown apart what should have been a very simple operation, and made it all suddenly very complicated.

In his relief at seeing Cliff and the injured man reach safety, Jim Gary almost forgot his own peril. The whine of a rifle bullet, and the stinging impact as it slapped within inches of him and showered him with rock pellets, warned him that he was still exposed to that marksman on the ridge. He whipped up his sixgun, threw a shot that came close enough to drive the man into cover. Then he changed position, hugging what protection the half-buried boulder could give him from that direction.

Down below it looked as though Webb Toland, in his determination, was about to rush the two Spur crewmen. Deliberately Gary fired. It was a long range for a revolver but in that clot of mounted men it wasn't hard to reach some target. He saw one of the riders lifted from his saddle and slammed to the ground. At the same moment, one of the Spur men—Cliff Frazer, most likely—started shooting.

That was enough for Toland's men. They turned and pulled back quickly for the protection of Buck Ridge, leaving their dead companion sprawled in the grass beside the fence. Silence returned then, broken by an uneasy stirring of the cattle; terrified by the gunfire, they might have tried to bolt from it except that it apparently was coming from every side.

Gary, bellying the dirt, checked the position of the rifleman but failed to find him. As he jacked empties from his six-shooter and reloaded from the loops in his belt, he called down to the pair trapped in the rocks below: "Hack? Cliff?"

Cliff Frazer answered. "You all right?"

"I'm doing fine. How's Hack making it?"

The hurt man answered for himself, his voice tight with pain but wholly defiant. "Got the bleeding stopped. Reckon a little old hole in my leg won't kill me. Damned if I'll let it, without I take a couple of them bastards along! Since when are they mixed in this fight, anyway?"

"It's a long story," Gary called back. "Just sit easy. Don't do anything foolish."

He wished he could tell them of the trump card they were holding. He couldn't, because Toland would be listening to every word. It didn't matter. Webb Toland's work was cut out for him, now. He was going to have to try and dispose of all three. And meanwhile, figuring from the time Fern Keating left town, it would certainly seem she'd have managed by now to reach Spur home ranch and warn her stepfather, and so get the crew started for here. Help should be only minutes away, if they could stick it out.

Only Jim Gary was not the man to sit and wait for help, when at any time young Frazer—or even Hack Bales, hurt as he was—might take it into his head to make some rash move, not realizing how things stood.

Then the rifleman on the ridge dropped another shot so close to him he knew the man must have changed into a better position. Gary waited no longer.

Tensed muscles drove him to his feet, during the instant the rifleman would need to lever a new shell into the breech. He caught a glimpse of his target and drove off a pair of shots as fast as he could work trigger. Though he fired instinctively, without time to aim, the second shot was lucky. The sharpshooter appeared to dive face forward into the brush, as a man might dive into deep water. He crashed from sight, and the rifle leaped from his hands to go skittering, end for end, down the slope, disappearing.

Gary saw this from a corner of his eye; he himself was already running, boots fighting the pitch and loose dirt of the hillside. With each step he cast ahead for some glimpse of his remaining enemies. Then, as he crested a slight hump and the whole flank of the ridge suddenly lay before him shagged with buckbrush and thick sage clumps, he saw the thing that brought him up short, in disbelief.

There was Webb Toland and Fern Keating, standing close, her face lifted to him and her hand laid against his chest in a way that suggested an astounding intimacy. Gary shook his head, for that first moment too stunned to think. Then the fact of her presence here descended full on him, like the crash of a wave breaking over his head.

Suddenly, half-guessed truths, things that had halfway suggested themselves to him last night as he knelt beside Paul Keating and saw the hating look he gave his wife as he died—all these hints began to drop into place. And one thing came through, with an appalling clarity: *If she's here with Toland, then she never took the message to Spur! You've been looking for help that isn't going to come!*

It was while he absorbed this, and adjusted his thinking to it, that he suddenly caught the drum of hoofs in the draw below. Looking, he saw a half-dozen riders filing up the trough between the ridges. Among them he recognized Burl Hoffman, and Vince Alcord's unmistakable, nearly deformed shape. They were heading for the rocks where Bales and Frazer were holed up. And they came from a direction that would take the pair on an unprotected flank.

Those two were doomed unless Gary could somehow manage to help them.

He drew a bead on Burl Hoffman but then lowered the gun, chagrined at knowing he had no target for a sixshooter. And as he debated what he could possibly do, a gunsear clicked behind him. A voice he didn't know said, "Don't try to use the gun, mister!"

XII

SLOWLY he turned. The man in black was a stranger, but he had been one of the group with Toland down there by the fence. Though Jim Gary didn't know him, the type was familiar enough. Like Gary himself, he was obviously the kind who made a living from the hire of his gun. Judging by the way he held it trained on Gary, he was undoubtedly good with it.

Jim Gary didn't drop his own gun. His chances were gone if he let himself be disarmed, and so he took the greater chance and tried for a shot, hurling himself to one side as he brought the weapon up. The black-clad gunman fired, with the first motion. Gary felt the bullet strike and was knocked bodily to the ground. But he kept his hold on the sixshooter and even as he landed, prone, his sights were on his opponent and he fired a second time, from there.

He saw the other jerk and whirl clear around, a convulsive pressure of his trigger-finger sending a last bullet winging wildly along the slope. But Jim Gary didn't see him fall. Blackness and pain swept over him. As he lay fighting it, he thought he heard a woman's scream mingle with the roar of the guns. He was too dazed, at that moment, to think clearly.

The pain was gathering itself now. He could feel it centering in the general region of his left arm and shoulder. Pushing to his knees, he looked down and saw the blood beginning to work through the fabric of his coat. But then he forgot his injury, as he became aware of gunfire beginning in the draw below him. Remembering the plight of the two men trapped there, he struggled to his feet.

What he saw astounded him.

More riders—a second, and larger bunch of them—had appeared from somewhere and were pouring in on Alcord and Hoffman and their crews. All at once the attackers found themselves outnumbered and under fire. Dust arose, mingling

131

with the fumes of burnt powder. Saddles emptied. Even as Gary watched, he saw guns flung down and arms raised in surrender.

It could mean only one thing: Spur! Yet he failed to understand for he knew that Fern Keating couldn't have warned them.

But that reminded him of Webb Toland, almost forgotten, in these past few minutes. He whipped around, hunting the man and finding no sign of any living person on that ridge except himself. Yet Toland could not have gone far. Not if he had a woman with him.

Quickly, ignoring the throb of his thawing shoulder wound, Jim Gary went looking, wading and crashing through waist-high clumps of brush that cloaked the hillside and held him back.

Under some scrub trees near the top of the ridge, he saw a clot of saddle horses and at once turned toward them. When he came upon Webb Toland, it was so unexpectedly that he almost overran him.

For Toland was on his knees, with Fern Keating cradled motionless against his breast. Gary, halting, stared at the two of them for a long moment before Toland seemed aware of his presence. Then the dark head lifted, the tawny eyes met Gary's, and they were clouded with grief. Webb Toland said, as though it were something he could not really believe, "My God! She's *dead!*"

Jim Gary saw the blood now, and remembered the scream that sounded on the heels of the black-clad gunman's second shot. A wild bullet, it must have streaked aimlessly along the hillside and found its target, quite by accident. He shook his head at the irony of it.

"Too bad," he said, without emotion. Then, gesturing with the point of the gun: "On your feet, Toland. I'm taking you with me."

Toland looked at the gun and at Gary's hard face. He said, "You're a cold devil, aren't you?" And when the other made no reply: "We can't just walk away and leave her lying here!"

"I'll see she's taken care of."

"No!" Toland clutched her tighter, one arm sliding under her body as in readiness to pick her up. "I'll carry her myself! Damn it, I can't think of her lying in the dirt—"

"She's not your responsibility," Jim Gary snapped coldly. "And she never was, whatever you two may have had between you while she was Paul Keating's wife! Now, get up from there."

Quietly Webb Toland answered, "I hope I see you in hell!" And his right hand slipped into sight, holding the gun he had managed to palm under cover of Fern's body. Toland slanted the weapon up at Gary and his face was a mask of hatred. But before he could fire, Gary triggered deliberately. He shot Toland in the chest and knocked him over backward. Gun smoking in his hand, he walked over and looked at the man.

Toland's arms were spread wide, empty hands plucking convulsively at the grass and weeds. He peered at Gary with dimming eyes. "Damn you!" he whispered. "I should have made sure and got you, last night, instead of your horse."

"Then it was you, there in the willows? And it was you that shot Keating?"

There was no answer. The tawny eyes glazed over. The man was dead.

By now, the last of Spur's enemies had surrendered. Matt Winship stared down from his saddle at Burl Hoffman and Vince Alcord, with a fine, flashing scorn. He seemed a different person from the beaten, dispirited man who had first hired, and then fired, Jim Gary. One would have said this attack had been the thing he needed to drag him out of an uncharacteristic lethargy. "I'd be in my rights," he said furiously, "to throw the book at you. Maybe I will, I ain't decided. But you damn well better walk easy!"

Vince Alcord cringed before his fury, and Hoffman said, flushing, "We was only trying to look after our interests. We don't want no syndicate on this range!"

"Syndicate?" Winship gave a snort. "Don't jump to conclusions. I ain't so damn sure there's gonna be any syndicate! I'm beginning to think Jim Gary had it straight, that it's time I got up off my hind end and fought for my rights!"

If he sensed the pleased surprise that went through his crewmen, the rancher failed to show it. He had caught sight of Jim Gary walking up, leading the horse someone had caught up for him. His bearded face held a scowl of alarm as he saw the blood on Gary's coat. "You took a bullet!"

Gary shook his head. "It's nothing much. Did Spur lose any men?"

"Nobody hurt to speak of, outside the hole in Hack Bales's leg, that is." Winship paused. "Gary, I'm thinking now I owe you an apology. You seen I was making a damn fool of myself, with that talk about quitting and selling out. I dunno what could have got into me! But I sure knew it was time to fight when that rider Tracy sent from town brought us the word of what was going on here!"

"Tracy sent the word?" Suddenly he could guess what had happened. With a woman's intuitive suspicion, she'd never really trusted Fern Keating. She must have decided to play safe, make doubly sure Spur got warning. Bless her for that!

"I got plenty to thank you for," Matt Winship went on, his deep voice heavy with embarrassment. "I'd like you to forget that firin' business. Spur still needs a good foreman, permanent. I'm asking you to come back."

"Thanks, Matt," Gary said and meant it. "I'd like to." But then he remembered, and he frowned. "I don't know, though. I'm afraid there's something else I've got to take care of—some unfinished business."

The other's black brows drew together. "You mean you're turning me down?"

"I'll have to see. I've made a promise. One I can't back out on. And it means that, right now, I have to be riding."

In a dead silence, they watched him turn and lift himself into the saddle. He winced, stretching his hurt shoulder. Matt Winship saw, and said, "You better let us do something about that, before you ride anywhere!"

He shook his head. Reining away, he caught Ed Saxon's eye. He rode over to the man, leaned to speak softly enough that no one else would hear. "Up on the ridge: Webb Toland, and Fern—both dead."

Astonishment and horror warped the other's face. *"Fern?"*

"I'm only beginning to guess at what it all adds up to. Damned if I know how you're going to break it to Matt!"

"That's all right. I'll think of something."

Gary thanked him with a nod. And thus, he rode from there—rode for town, and the rendezvous he had promised Boyd and Asa Plank.

His left shoulder throbbed dully, but the wadded handkerchief he'd stuffed inside his coat seemed to have absorbed the bleeding. He shoved the hand into his waist belt and let that support the weight of the arm and keep it motionless.

A kind of depression rode him, a letdown after the tensions of gunplay. His entire battered body seemed to be one tired ache. But there was more to it than that. These last days, since immersing himself in the affairs of this range, had worked their change in him. He'd begun unknowingly to put down roots. As he'd told Tracy Bannister, it was a new experience for him to feel needed.

Now Spur's worst troubles appeared settled. There was the offer of a permanent job. And finally, there was Tracy—that moment in the hotel lobby, when her kiss had made it certain that, whatever else happened, he was never going to forget her.

Yet in the face of all this he was riding to meet the Planks! He drew his gun, thinking to replace the spent shells, but knowing that in a showdown he would never use it against that pair to whom he owed his life. He shrugged and shoved it back again. Perhaps this was crazy, perhaps it was a kind of suicide. Or on the other hand, maybe it was only justice; a man with his past didn't deserve such rewards.

He took the fording where the road crossed Antler Creek. Topping out on the south bank, he climbed a slight rise in the trail, and saw the two horsemen approaching, a mile down the road. Even at that distance, he recognized the Planks. They were coming to meet him!

Something rose in Gary, nearly choking him. He settled it and then rode on. His hand was steady enough on the rein, his jaw set firm with the determination to have this out, to whatever hard ending.

Slowly the distance narrowed. They were close enough now that he could see their faces—grim, implacable, expressionless. Their guns rode their holsters, their gunhands hanging awkwardly near the jutting grips. Presently, when only yards remained to separate them, Jim Gary hauled up. His horse tossed its head, then settled. Wind across the sun-scorched grass fingered its mane, fanned the brim of Gary's hat, touched his cheek. Motionless, he waited.

Still Boyd and Asa Plank came on. They edged their horses slightly apart, now. So they meant to take him from both sides, put him between them. . . .

They drew nearer, still at that same unbroken, plodding pace. Now they were abreast of his horse, one on either side.

They rode straight past. Their eyes did not even touch his face or appear to see him!

Astounded, Jim Gary whirled his horse. Feeling that he was the victim of some kind of trick, he stared at their backs as the distance continued to widen. Unable at last to hold it in, he called harshly, "What the hell is this? Where do you think you're going?"

They pulled rein, then. They looked back, without turning their horses. For a moment, neither spoke. It was big Boyd Plank who answered him, in a strange, flat tone.

"Ask the girl. That Tracy Bannister—she's quite a woman. And quite a talker! She told us things we hadn't heard. About Lane, and how you come to kill him." He hesitated, scowling. "Could all be a lie, of course. But *she* believes it. And, by damn, she near convinced us!"

"We wouldn't want to make any mistakes," Asa said. "She told us you been cutting quite a swath in this part of the country. Looks like we could have been wrong in the kind of man you are, and I reckon we both knew Lane wasn't no angel!

"Anyway, killing you wouldn't bring him back. And that girl seems to think a lot of you, Gary. You just better the hell be worthy of her!"

Without another word, they were gone—toward Mogul Valley, turning their backs on the revenge they could have taken. Jim Gary let the cramped breath from his lungs slowly. For a long moment he watched that pair grow small against the immensity of rangeland.

He spoke to his horse, then, and rode on—toward Antler, and the girl who had given him a new life, and a new beginning.

Clement Hardin was a pseudonym of **D(wight) B(ennett) Newton** and is the author of a number of notable Western novels. Born in Kansas City, Missouri, Newton went on to complete work for a Master's degree in history at the University of Missouri. From the time he first discovered Max Brand in Street and Smith's *Western Story Magazine*, he knew he wanted to be an author of Western fiction. He began contributing Western stories and novelettes to the Red Circle group of Western pulp magazines published by Newsstand in the late 1930s. During the Second World War, Newton served in the US Army Engineers and fell in love with the central Oregon region when stationed there. He would later become a permanent resident of that state and Oregon frequently serves as the locale for many of his finest novels. As a client of the August Lenniger Literary Agency, Newton found that every time he switched publishers he was given a different byline by his agent. This complicated his visibility. Yet in notable novels from *Range Boss* (1949), the first original novel ever published in a modern paperback edition, through his impressive list of titles for the Double D series from Doubleday, *The Oregon Rifles, Crooked River Canyon*, and *Disaster Creek* among them, he produced a very special kind of Western story. What makes it so special is the combination of characters who seem real and about whom a reader comes to care a great deal and Newton's fundamental humanity, his realization early on (perhaps because of his study of history) that little that happened in the West was ever simple but rather made desperately complicated through the conjunction of numerous opposed forces working at cross purposes. Yet, through all of the turmoil on the frontier, a basic human decency did emerge. It was this which made the American frontier experience so profoundly unique and which produced many of the remarkable human beings to be found in the world of Newton's Western fiction.